The Schoo

The boo... dog on the towpath. It lay, face downwards, in the ditch between the towpath and the massive stone-wall of the cutting. The man telephoned Central Police Station. Detective Sergeant Hammond and Detective Constable Symons were first on the scene.

Hammond was short for a policeman; he wore a shabby raincoat and a cloth cap; he had a thin, sad face with small, bright eyes. A disillusioned terrier. His companion was young, good looking and inclined to be dim.

The body rested on a cushion of brambles which choked the ditch. Hammond eyed it with disfavour because it was going to spoil his Saturday.

"He must have been here all night."

The dead man was short and tubby; his clothes were sodden from the rain but they seemed to be of good quality. A lightweight raincoat, grey, worsted trousers with a fine purple stripe, grey suède shoes and silk socks to match. His head was bare and his thinning hair was dark. His right temple had been smashed in by a powerful blow and was crusted with blood.

Other titles in the Walker British Mystery Series

W.J. BURLEY

The
Schoolmaster

WALKER AND COMPANY · NEW YORK

First published in the United States of America
in 1977 by the Walker Publishing Company, Inc.

This paperback edition first published in 1984.

ISBN 0-8027-3057-4

Library of Congress Catalog Card Number; 76-52297

Printed in the United States of America

10 9 8 7 6 5 4 3 2 1

Chapter One

THREE O'CLOCK IN the afternoon, the last period of the day. Arthur Milton, due to teach his upper-sixth history set, paused in the corridor outside the classroom to hear what was being said. He had an almost morbid desire to know what his pupils said about him and he excused his eavesdropping on the ground that he never made use of what he heard.

'Hell! I've left his Fisher at home again. He's already asked me for it twice.' That was John Rickard.

'What are we supposed to be doing this afternoon?' A girl's voice, a self-conscious drawl—Rita Morley.

'He's going through our essays on the Congress of Vienna.' Another girl's voice, unidentified.

'God! I only did two sides, he'll screw me.' Rita again.

'No dear, I shouldn't think so, not our Milly.'

'Idiot! I was speaking metaphorically.'

'What's that? Can anybody do it?'

Milton went in and took his seat under the blackboard. Seven girls and six boys—thirteen candidates for History A-level. He kept his numbers up, not because he was popular but because he got results.

It was raining and the windows were obscured by water streaming down the panes. There was a curious feeling of isolation and, at the same time, of intimacy; a family atmosphere, but Milton knew that he had no part in it.

'This afternoon I want to go over your essays on the Congress of Vienna.' He tapped the pile of scripts on the desk in front of him. 'None of you has done justice to the role of Talleyrand in the negotiations....'

His voice was high-pitched and when he spoke with any enthusiasm it had a bell-like quality. With his perfect diction and calculated pauses he sounded like Gielgud reading Shakespeare.

'In 1815 Talleyrand at sixty-one was already a dinosaur, a living fossil. Think of it—by trimming his sails to each change of wind he had survived storm and tempest from the days of Louis XVI (who made him a bishop) to the second Bourbon restoration.' A pause to allow this to sink in. 'The man was an enigma. Carlyle said of him that he lived in falsehood and on falsehood yet was not a false man. On the other hand De Quincey saw him as "that rather middling bishop but very eminent knave"....'

He distributed the essay scripts with a dry word to each of his pupils: 'Your argument, Elaine, might have more force if Metternich really had been a Russian as you seem to believe ... Your essay was bread-and-butter stuff, John, you can do better ... This must have taken you all of twenty minutes, Rita; I sometimes wonder how you manage to fit my work into your busy life....'

The lesson purred on its tranquil, boring course; the rain increased and battered on the windows; Milton looked in vain for some animation in the faces of his pupils and told thin, crusty jokes at which nobody laughed. At last it was five minutes to four and the bell went for the end of school. They clattered out while Milton remained seated at his desk making careful notes in his class record. One boy, Alan Wilson, remained behind.

Wilson was tall and fair with delicate, girlish features and pink-and-white colouring; he stood by Milton's desk, waiting. This was only his second term at the school.

'What is it?'

Milton did not look up.

The boy was holding his essay, uneasily determined. 'You only gave me a beta-minus....'

'I gave you what your essay was worth.'

'Yes, but I wondered if you could tell me what's wrong with it?'

Milton finally raised his eyes to look at the boy and frowned. 'If you are really serious about the Oxford entrance, Wilson, it's time you developed a greater critical faculty. Work at this level is not simply a matter of collecting and regurgitating facts and I am quite sure that they will look for a more analytical approach than you have shown in your work for me.'

6

'I try to weigh things up—I read a lot around the subject....'

'I don't doubt it, but the thing is to understand what you read and to make use of it in your judgements.'

Milton gathered up his papers and slipped them into his briefcase.

'This is your second term with us and to be frank I'm inclined to think that your old school gave you a somewhat exaggerated view of your ability.'

The boy flushed; Milton saw it and made a half-hearted attempt to draw the sting. 'I shouldn't let it worry you unduly: there are other universities and I have no doubt that we shall persuade one of them to take you.'

Wilson said nothing and after a moment he turned away and went out, closing the door behind him.

Milton remained seated for some time, staring at the desk top; a barely visible tic trembled in one corner of his mouth. Finally he picked up his case and paced with long, slow strides down the polished corridor to the staff common-room. Over the years he had acquired a magisterial walk which was as much a part of him as his dark suits and the rigidity of his routine.

Some members of staff had gone home, others were at various meetings or supervising after-school activities, a few lingered in the common-room drinking coffee and putting the world to rights. He was conscious of them watching him while he collected books from his locker and he knew that as soon as the door closed behind him one of them would make some slighting remark which would provoke a general laugh at his expense. He felt set apart; an object observed, criticised and commented on by staff and pupils alike. He wished that he could shut himself away, find some absorbing task which he could pursue alone and never have to face them again. Instead he buried himself ever more deeply in routine, obsessively anxious to avoid any departure which might draw attention and comment. His clerical-grey suits, quiet ties and white shirts; his walk, his studied manner, his formal method of teaching—through all these it seemed that he tried to be like certain timid animals who, by a combination of cryptic colouration and behaviour, strive to escape notice.

The school car-park was swept by rain; he put up his umbrella and set out across the streaming tarmac. His daughter, Elizabeth, was waiting for him in the car. At sixteen she was studying biology, chemistry and physics at A-level in the hope of going to university to read medicine.

'Have you been waiting long?'

'Not long.'

'You must have got wet crossing the car-park.'

'Not very.'

'You should have waited in school.'

She was a pretty girl with chestnut hair, long and silky, half hiding her face which was rounded and lightly freckled.

Milton strapped himself in and started the engine. With great deliberation he put the car into gear, let in the clutch; the car leapt forward and stalled. At the second attempt he was more successful, they moved out of the car-park and joined a stream of traffic going northward out of the city. A van in front sent up jets of muddy water and the windscreen wipers were scarcely able to cope.

'What homework have you got?'

'A biology question and some practical physics to write up.'

'No chemistry?'

'No.'

Milton was late in braking when the traffic stopped for the lights and the car skidded a little on the wet surface.

'You seem to get very little chemistry homework.'

'The same as the rest.'

'I don't doubt that, but is it enough?'

'I suppose so. Mr Green knows what he's doing.'

'I hope so, but Mr Green is a very young man. Perhaps I should have a word....'

'No, daddy—no, *please*.' In her anxiety she put her hand on his arm as he reached for the gear lever.

'Elizabeth!'

'I'm sorry, but you won't say anything, will you?'

'I'll think about it.'

They came to the roundabout in silence. Elizabeth was staring out of the side window though there was little to be seen through the film of condensation. Although he made the journey daily Milton was in the wrong lane and he had to turn off across the line of traffic. A car hooted.

'Oaf!' Milton muttered through his teeth.

They had left the main traffic flow and were in the maze of roads which served the northern suburbs.

'Elizabeth,' he waited until she had turned to face him, 'I would rather you didn't make a special friend of Alan Wilson.'

'Why not?' Her voice betrayed a sudden tension.

'There are plenty of other very nice boys in our sixth, why does it have to be him?'

'But why not Alan? What have you got against him?'

He was aware of rising irritation but he controlled it. 'I didn't say that I have anything against him.'

'Then why mustn't I go out with him? I'm surely old enough to pick my friends or at least be told why I shouldn't.'

Milton gripped the steering wheel more firmly. 'I don't want to get involved in an argument, Elizabeth, it's just that I think you've been seeing rather too much of Wilson lately and I'm asking you to be reasonable and not to see him so often.'

'And I think I've a right to know why.'

Milton did not answer. He made two left turns in quick succession and entered a road of detached houses with neat, unfenced lawns separating them from the pavement.

'Does he ever mention me?'

'Why should he?'

Milton's voice acquired a sharper edge. 'I asked you a question: does he ever speak of me?'

'Not much. He thinks you don't like him and it seems that he's right.'

He turned the car into a drive and pulled up in front of the green drop-door of his garage.

'Satisfied?'

'Don't be impertinent, Elizabeth.'

She got out and raised the garage door for him to drive in, then she collected her briefcase from the back seat and went indoors without another word.

When he got out of the car he stood still for a moment, breathing deeply until he felt more relaxed, then he locked the garage door from the inside and went through into the house. He hung his coat in the hall cupboard and put his books and briefcase in his study.

Every evening the same routine; he would wash his hands in the downstairs cloakroom before joining his wife in the kitchen to kiss her on the cheek.

'Where's Elizabeth?'

Jean did not turn round. 'Gone upstairs to do her homework.'

Jean Milton was younger than her husband, still under forty. She was on the short side with a well rounded figure, still attractive to men. Her butcher-blue, striped apron emphasised the smallness of her waist and her movements as she worked had a precise delicacy which fascinated him. When they were first married, watching her work in the kitchen sometimes excited him so much that he wanted to take her there and then. But he never did.

'Why is she in such a rush to do her homework tonight?'

Jean was rolling out pastry with a blue glass rolling-pin. 'She's going out.'

'With Alan Wilson?'

'They're going to the folk club.'

'She said nothing to me about it.'

'Why should she? Surely she's old enough to have an occasional evening out with a boy-friend without having a family conference about it.'

Milton put his hands into the pockets of his jacket, a sure sign that he was digging in.

'I'm not at all happy about her going round with that boy.'

'Why not? I thought he seemed a nice, sensible lad.'

'I don't like him.' He added after a moment, 'Why does it have to be him?'

'You'd be the same about anybody she went round with, the trouble is that you're jealous.'

'*Jealous?*'

'Of any boy who takes her fancy.'

'That is a disgusting thing to say!'

Jean laughed, a gurgling sound which seemed to well up inside her. 'There's nothing disgusting about it: fathers are jealous of their daughter's boy-friends just as mothers are jealous of the girls their sons bring home. It's natural.'

10

'Natural? I think it's obscene!'

He stood, tense and rigid. As always he was genuinely distressed when she put a sexual interpretation on his attitudes. She had always been outspoken in such matters and she had brought up Elizabeth to be the same. In the early days of their marriage she had made no secret of her pleasure in sex, often taking the lead and indulging in words and actions which shocked him. She would ask him embarrassing questions, teasing him....

'Well, that wasn't a bad effort for a beginner. *Are* you a beginner?'

'I don't know what you mean.'

'It's simple enough—did you have women before you met me?'

She was laughing at him, but he could not respond in the same light vein.

'No.'

'But you were twenty-six, how did you manage?' She was looking at him, smiling, relaxed and unselfconscious. 'Did you...?'

He took refuge in irritation. 'I don't like this sort of discussion.'

She was unabashed. 'You're a very funny man. I thought most men enjoyed talking about sex. I read somewhere that the average man thinks about sex at least once every ten minutes.'

'Rubbish!'

To be precise he had not been so much shocked as frightened by her behaviour. There are limits beyond which it is unsafe to go, invisible barriers which, once crossed, may transform a man into a beast without scruple or control. Total abandonment. Jean had never understood; she treated sex as a rather jolly domestic pet with whom it was safe to romp and play and tease.

It was now six months since they had shared the same bed. Jean had gradually withdrawn herself and he had accepted the situation. In fact, he achieved a certain satisfaction in self-denial; he did not smoke or drink and sexual abstinence was just another challenge. Sometimes it seemed that by his

11

ritual behaviour and sacrifices he was seeking to placate his gods.

'I have rather a lot of marking to do. I'd better start before the meal.'

Jean was lining a shallow dish with pastry, pressing it gently down into the crinkled rim. 'Oh, I forgot. Ralph Barton rang, he wants you to ring him back.'

'What about?'

'The choral society, I suppose. He didn't say.'

They had their meal at six-thirty. The dining room looked out over the back garden through french windows, but the rain was streaming down the window panes making it impossible to see through them. The dining suite had been specially made—reproduction Sheraton—a folly in which he had invested the whole of a legacy from his mother. He wanted their home to have a certain distinction, an elegance that would be visible evidence of its stability and security. The gas fire made a faint, continuous hissing sound which had come to be associated with mealtimes for they talked little. He liked to concentrate on his food, which he ate somewhat greedily so that he finished each course before Jean or Elizabeth and was forced to wait for the next. It was traditional that Elizabeth served the sweet course and made the coffee.

'I shall have to go out this evening after all. I telephoned Ralph Barton and he's called a special meeting of the committee.'

'Trouble?'

'At our last meeting we agreed to do Tippett's *A Child of Our Time*. Alec Johns missed that meeting because he was away on a business trip, but now he's back and he thinks we should stick with Handel for another year. He feels quite strongly and he's making a fuss. It really is annoying.'

'But I thought you wanted to do something of Handel's?'

'I did, but the decision was made and I hate uncertainty.'

Elizabeth brought in the percolator and coffee cups on a tray which she placed in front of her father.

'Your mother tells me that you are off to the folk club this evening.'

'Yes.'

'Then I hope you won't be late back. Ten o'clock is plenty

late enough when you have another school day tomorrow.'
He waited for a reply which did not come. 'Don't you agree?'

'Yes, daddy.'

The irony of her inflection escaped him. 'Good!' He turned
to his wife. 'Are you going out this evening, Jean?'

'You know that I never go out on Thursdays.'

They were living separate lives with little more than shared
meals in common. Two years ago Jean had taken a part-time
job in an insurance office. At that time their social life, such
as it was, had been shared; now they went out together only
when a school occasion required it and not to do so would
have given rise to comment.

One evening six months ago Jean had said, 'You're not
going out this evening, are you?'

'No, why?'

'A friend at the office has invited me out for a meal. I've
put everything ready for you and Elizabeth. . . .'

A certain delicacy, or perhaps a vague fear, had stopped
him from asking questions then and he had never questioned
her since. She had soon settled to a routine; Monday, Wednesday and Saturday evenings. To an outsider it would have
seemed incredible that no reference of any kind was made
to where she went or what she did. She would say simply,
'I'll leave everything ready. . . .'

He was not a fool. He did not imagine that Jean was spending her time with a woman friend, but as long as the facts
were not put into words he could live with them. Then, one
morning during coffee in the staff-room, Bates, the headmaster, had said,

'You missed a jolly good meal last night, Arthur.'

'Indeed?' He looked vague.

'Didn't Jean tell you? The new place in King Street . . . Jean
was there with her brother. As a matter of fact we had a
drink together.'

Bates sipped his coffee. Milton said nothing.

'Nice chap; Carol was quite taken with him. Looks prosperous.'

'Yes, I think he is.'

Bates was sly and his wife was a bitch. '. . . With her
brother'—had the words been spoken with a certain emphasis?

13

Whether they had or not, Milton now had evidence he would rather have been without. He decided reluctantly that he must speak to Jean, but the right moment evaded him and he had not spoken. Nothing changed.

The meeting of the choral society dragged on until half-past ten and it was nearly eleven when he got home. Jean and Elizabeth were in the lounge. Both wore their dressing gowns and they were drinking cocoa, seated on the rug in front of the gas fire. Jean liked to cultivate a girl-to-girl relationship with her daughter.

'Want some cocoa?'

'No, thank you.'

He was conscious of having interrupted something. Elizabeth's eyes were red and she was not as adept at covering her feelings as her mother.

'How did it go?' Jean was bright and brittle.

'Oh, they decided to go on with the Tippett.'

'Good, if that's what you wanted.'

They slept in the same room though in separate beds and Jean made no attempt to hide her body from him. Except in winter she slept naked and she would often spend several minutes naked in front of the mirror, brushing her hair or applying creams to her skin.

'What's the matter with Elizabeth?'

'Nothing, why?'

'She'd been crying.'

'Oh, it's nothing much. Like all girls of her age she's got her problems.'

For Jean, this was unusually evasive; she seldom missed an opportunity to discuss the intimate details of Elizabeth's physical and emotional life.

'Anything to do with me?'

'No, nothing.'

She stood for a moment looking down at him before climbing into her bed.

'Good night, Arthur.' She was smiling.

Was she being provocative? Was it an invitation?

'Good night, Jean.'

Next morning the rain had gone and the sun was shining.

14

The trees in the copse behind the house were still in full leaf, though green had given place to reds and browns and the fall would soon begin. He felt mildly exhilarated and as he got the car out of the garage he was humming to himself. Jean and Elizabeth were at the gate; Elizabeth got in front with him, Jean in the back.

There was a feeling of constraint which he could not understand. Although they rarely said much it was unusual to do the journey in silence. Jean seemed to be aware of the difference and made an effort at conversation.

'I've left Mrs Watson's money on the drainer.'

Mrs Watson was the woman who came each morning to do the cleaning. Jean left her money on the drainer every Friday but did not usually mention it.

'I suppose you've got your dinner money, Elizabeth?'

'Yes.'

'Look! They're putting up traffic lights. What on earth do they want lights there for?'

'It's going to be a controlled pedestrian crossing.'

They had to make a detour through the city centre to drop Jean. At lunchtime she would come home by bus.

When he was alone with Elizabeth he decided to probe.

'Lovely morning, isn't it?'

'Yes.'

'Did you have a good time at the folk club last night?'

'It was all right.'

'What's the matter?'

'Nothing is the matter, why do you ask?'

For a time he was involved with a traffic hold-up at a complicated road junction. When they were clear he tried again.

'Elizabeth, if I come the heavy father sometimes it's only because I want you to work and get good A-levels so that you can go to university and become a doctor.'

'I know, daddy, don't worry.'

He was surprised by the warmth in her voice.

'That's what you want too, isn't it?'

'Of course it is. You don't have to worry about me, not ever. I shan't do anything silly.'

'I'm sure you won't.'

He was deeply moved. It was the first time in years that

they had come so close to an expression of real feeling.

As she got out of the car in the school car-park he called after her,

'Have a good day!'

She waved to him.

It was a school day like any other, yet there was something special about it. For one thing it was glorious weather, one of those days when it is difficult to believe that winter is just round the corner. The sun shone, the air sparkled and the birds were almost deceived into believing that spring had returned. The boys and girls were affected; they were quieter, more thoughtful; seeming to look at their friends and their surroundings with new eyes as though seeing them afresh.

Milton taught his classes as usual but his manner was different: lighter, more buoyant. In the back of his mind he was thinking: 'It may be possible, life isn't over at forty-four.' He recalled the smile his wife had given him the night before, enigmatic and mysterious, as she climbed naked into bed. And he remembered this morning's brief exchange with Elizabeth. . . .

He made a point of getting away promptly at four o'clock and as he crossed the car-park he was looking forward to seeing Elizabeth sitting in the car waiting for him. But the car was empty and he remembered with a stab of disappointment that it was Friday. On Fridays Elizabeth had a hockey match and she would catch the bus home.

He was tempted to stay and watch the match and take her home afterwards but he was wary of upsetting her arrangements. The last thing he wanted now was to seem to spy on her. He went home by way of the Grove and in the florist's by the cathedral he bought some white chrysanthemums.

As he turned into their road he saw his house in the sunshine. A detached house in a good neighbourhood, solidly built, well maintained, and his. Free, as the lawyers say, of all encumbrances. He decided that before dinner he would cut the grass in front, probably for the last time until spring.

He put the car away and, carrying his briefcase and the flowers, went through into the house.

The kitchen was empty and there was no sign of a meal in preparation. There was a note on the drainer but that was from

16

the cleaning woman and said, simply, 'No bags for the Hoover'.

He put the flowers in the sink, went to the bottom of the stairs and called, 'Jean, are you up there?'

He wondered if she had come home feeling unwell and gone to lie down. He went upstairs to their bedroom but there was no one. He felt puzzled rather than concerned. There would be some simple explanation, but he would have expected her to leave a note or to have telephoned the school office. Then he remembered the bread. Jean bought bread from a small private bakery near her office and, as it was Friday, she would have brought home the week-end supply. But the bread-bin held only the tail-end of a loaf. Did that mean that she had not been home at all?

The sun was streaming through the windows at the back of the house seeming to emphasise the stillness. Of course it was possible that she had had an accident but her handbag was a virtual filing system for documents of various sorts. They would have let him know. The grandfather clock in the hall which had a brass face showed half past five. Elizabeth would be home soon and the thought cheered him. It would be more sensible if he set about getting some sort of meal. As soon as he started to busy himself in the kitchen he would hear Jean's key in the lock, there would be a flurry of explanation, an account of misunderstanding and frustration, and in a few minutes everything would be back to normal.

But he did not go into the kitchen; instead he went into the lounge and stood by the window, where he could see the corner round which she must come. He caught sight of the top of a brown head, bobbing up and down, just visible above the hedge of the corner house. He held his breath. It could be Jean, but it wasn't; a fat, plain little woman, nothing like her. A car arrived at the corner but turned in the other direction, a van, another car, a man walking. . . . He would do what he should have done before, telephone her office. The number was on the pad by the telephone. He dialled and listened to the ringing tone for a long time but there was no answer. He had left it too late, everybody had gone home.

Elizabeth should have come by now; she was usually in by a quarter to six but it was possible that she had missed the

17

bus. He would put the chrysanthemums in water and while he was doing it....

It was odd; the house was beginning to look like a stage set waiting for the action to begin. He switched on the television and stood still while it warmed up.

'... The Prime Minister said that we must be on our guard against mistaking the bleating of a noisy minority for the authentic voice of the British people.'

He switched off.

It was absurd to become worked up and tense yet, against his will, he was beginning to behave as though his smallest action was of great significance, almost as though he might be called to account. The grandfather clock in the hall struck six. He was moving about the house without any clear purpose, in a strangely diffident and tentative way as though he had no right to be there.

In a modern city, in reach of a telephone, of public transport, of taxis.... If she had not come home at lunchtime then she had been missing for several hours.

He let himself out by the front door, leaving it on the latch, and walked across the grass to his right-hand neighbour, Mrs Lambert. Her husband was a sales representative and away most of the week, so she had all the time in the world to keep an eye on everything that went on. Jean credited her with built-in radar and X-ray eyes.

With a last look towards the corner Milton rang the bell. The glass door opened almost at once and Mrs Lambert appeared, as though she had been waiting for him. She was lean and sharp featured, with a hard little mouth which she opened as little as possible when she spoke.

'Oh, Mr Milton!' She was ingratiating but her tiny smile was not convincing.

'I wondered if you had seen my wife or if she had left a message?'

'I haven't seen her since before lunch, I'm afraid.'

'You saw her then?'

She looked at him with greater interest. 'Oh, yes, she arrived home just after twelve in a taxi. I thought it was unusual, I mean, she's never home before half past one and she always comes on the bus.'

Milton hated having to put himself in the hands of this woman, to admit by implication that he did not understand his wife's conduct.

'You didn't see her go out again?'

'But I did. She kept the taxi waiting, nearly half-an-hour, then she came out with three suitcases; the taxi man had to help her.'

She paused to give Milton time to comment but when he said nothing she went on: 'I thought to myself, she's had a call at the office, somebody ill in the family.'

'I see.'

'Fancy her not leaving a message! I expect she phoned the school and they forgot to tell you, but she's sure to ring tonight. I shouldn't worry.'

The muffled but insistent ringing of a telephone suddenly acquired significance for him. He dashed across the grass to his own door, fumbled with the catch and entered the hall just as the ringing stopped. But he picked up the receiver and spoke into it foolishly then he sat on the stairs with his head in his hands. His throat was constricted and his eyes were smarting. He felt as an animal must feel when it is being cruelly and pointlessly teased. His heart thumped wildly and he had a hot, tingling sensation in the top of his head.

'Oh, God, let her come now.'

But he had little hope left.

Where could she have gone with the suitcases? The Lambert woman's theory about illness in the family sounded plausible but Jean had no family. She was an only child and when he married her both her parents had been dead for years. A vague collection of uncles had never made any contact.

He went upstairs to look in the wardrobe. Most of her clothes were gone.

He was being forced to a conclusion which he found almost incredible; she had left him, simply walked out.

And Elizabeth was still not at home. Could it be that she had gone with her mother? He remembered finding them together the previous night, sitting on the rug in front of the gas fire. Elizabeth had been crying. He remembered too Jean's smile when she wished him good night.

Although he had never doubted that Jean was having an

affair with another man he had never once considered the possibility that she would leave him. To be more exact, he had not thought it possible that she would leave her home. She had been twenty-two when he married her. Her parents had died in an accident when she was fourteen and for four years she had lived with a maiden aunt who treated her like an unpaid servant. At eighteen, when she had been working for two years, she left the aunt and shared a flat with two other girls. But that had not worked either and during the next four years—until they were married—she had tried lodgings, a bed-sitter and another attempt at sharing, this time with an older woman who turned out to be a lesbian.

He suspected at the time that she had married him for a home—a proper home—but he had not minded, for he thought himself immeasurably lucky to have got hold of this young, attractive girl. When they moved into their first house she had taken to it with a fierce possessiveness which had never wavered. Once, with unaccustomed humour, he had said, 'I suppose I just go with the house, like a cat.'

Seven o'clock, and he was pacing about like a caged animal. The telephone rang when he was by the kitchen sink and he dashed out into the hall, banging his knee against the kitchen door.

'479836 ... Hullo ... Hullo!'

He could hear movement at the other end.

'This is Jean, Arthur, I'm—'

'Jean! Where are you? I've been so worried—'

Her voice was unsteady yet determined. 'I know, I tried to get you earlier but there was no reply. I'm sorry, Arthur, but I've left you. I know it must be a shock and I should have warned you but I hadn't the courage. You would have tried to persuade me out of it and it wouldn't have done any good—'

'Jean—'

'No, you must listen. I know I've not been fair to you but I'm in love with another man and it's now or never. I've enough of my life in front of me to make a fresh start and that's what I'm doing—'

'But Jean—'

'No, Arthur, let me finish. You don't need me, Arthur, you never have. I'm not blaming you for that but what I'm saying

20

is that you'll soon get over it—once you've got a new routine.'

'But where are you?'

'I'm not going to tell you that, not now. When we've both had a day or two to come to terms with ourselves I'll get in touch again.'

'But what about Elizabeth?'

'She's with me. She had to make a choice, poor girl, but she can change her mind if she wants to—I'm not trying to hold her against her will. In any case you can talk to her yourself when she goes to school on Monday.'

She was speaking rapidly, trying to stop him getting a word in.

'I know I'm being selfish, Arthur, I don't deny that. But we've only got one life to live and I've been lucky enough to have a second chance of happiness. Try not to think too badly of me.'

There was a click and the line was dead.

He continued to hold the receiver. He even shouted foolishly, pleadingly, into the mouthpiece. 'Jean! Jean! ...' Then he dropped it back on its rest.

It was odd. His emotions were so mixed that he wanted to cry with bewilderment and frustration. Yet within minutes he had adopted an attitude which grossly over-simplified his feelings: he became outraged.

After eighteen years! What had he done? Hadn't he always been considerate and tolerant? Perhaps that was the real cause of the trouble, he'd been too tolerant, too long suffering....

He was angry, but his anger did nothing to fill the emptiness inside, an emptiness which was almost physical, which brought him to the point of nausea.

He walked round the house aimlessly, picking up things and putting them down again. He wanted to smash something, but that would have been too much out of character; that sham character of muted colours and passionless judgements which he had contrived so painfully but so thoroughly that it had almost become his real self.

'I'm being selfish ... Try not to think too badly of me....' What did she expect? Sympathy? Congratulations? He was so tense that he would find himself holding his breath. His heartbeat would become slower and slower until it thumped like

21

a great hammer in his chest and he would begin to feel dizzy. Then he would breathe, the tension would ease and the whole thing would start over again.

'But we've only got one life to live. . . .' What about his life?

The house was beginning to feel like a prison, but where could he go? He wished that he was a drinking man with a circle of acquaintances in some pub, but apart from the occasional glass of sherry he had not touched alcohol since his student days.

He needed people around him, people who would not ask questions.

It all came back to sex. Jean wanted a man who would encourage her in bawdy talk, respond in kind to her sexual teasing and finally throw off all restraint. She must have found such a man.

He had heard guarded talk from one or two of his colleagues about their wives. Little grouses only half expressed and spoken jestingly.

'When all else fails Jill has a headache.'

'If Di gives me the least encouragement I know it must be leap year.'

Weren't they normal women?

It was getting dark, there were bars of cloud above the copse, blue-black against the pale green sky which here and there was flushed with pink.

By now Jean would have been round the house and drawn all the curtains. Lights would be on in two or three of the rooms. Elizabeth would be upstairs doing her homework, he would be in his study marking or reading, Jean would be sitting on the rug in the lounge watching television or sewing.

He felt a catch in his throat. But why? Had he been happy in this daily round which had the regularity of a time-table?

He had eaten nothing since school lunch so he went into the kitchen and opened cupboards at random. By chance he came across a bottle of brandy somebody had given them, which Jean used for flavouring her puddings and trifles. He tipped three fingers into a tumbler and took it into the lounge. He lit the gas fire and settled in an easy chair.

Looking back it seemed so plain. He had seen the way his

22

colleagues looked at Jean when they were together. He knew his reputation as a man who lived by routine, dry, unbending, lacking warmth. Then they looked at Jean. However she dressed she looked lightly clad; however correct her behaviour she seemed to be inviting some approach—not actively, but passively, like a cream cake waiting to be eaten.

Was it any wonder they marvelled that the marriage could have lasted so long? Because they did, and he knew it, but until now the fact had not disturbed him but had given him a quiet confidence. It was like having a Swiss bank account.

The brandy was beginning to take effect. It made his lips tingle and his throat burn but took care of the emptiness inside.

What made him most angry was the secrecy; she had treated him like a child.

'But where are you?'

'I'm not going to tell you that now. When we've both had a day or two to come to terms with ourselves I'll get in touch again.'

Well, he would find out for himself. He had the week-end. He finished the brandy and went to fetch the bottle. He had to move cautiously now, because it was so dark and he had not switched on any lights. He could not stand the mute regard of all the things they had lived with for eighteen years.

By the time he went to bed his head was swimming and he had to hold on to both banisters. He threw off his coat and trousers, leaving them in a heap on the floor, and fell into bed wearing his shirt and underpants.

Chapter Two

HE WOKE ABRUPTLY and at once he was aware of two things which were abnormal: day-light flooding into the bedroom because the curtains had not been drawn, and the fact that he was wearing his shirt and underpants instead of pyjamas. An uneasy feeling of crisis crystallised into recollection. His mouth was dry and he had a dull ache at the base of his skull. He looked across at Jean's bed, which was empty and undisturbed.

He got out and went to the bathroom, feeling unsteady on his legs. He drank half a tumbler of water with two aspirins and took a shower which made him feel better. Then he put on his dressing gown and went downstairs. The grandfather clock showed a quarter to eight. Of one thing he had been certain, that he would not sleep; but the brandy had taken care of that.

There was post on the mat with the morning paper: a circular for Jean, a letter for Elizabeth from her friend in Lyons and a packet of stuff from the examining board for whom he did some marking. He put it all on the hall table unopened. At some time the previous evening or during the night he must have made up his mind what he would do, for he had no doubt now and the fact reassured him.

He made toast from the stale piece of bread, all that was left in the bread bin, but when he came to look for the butter all he had was in the refrigerator, as hard as a brick. He managed to scrape some off and melt it on the toast, and with a cup of instant coffee sat down to breakfast, his paper propped against the milk jug.

"Strikers Refuse Arbitration".

Yesterday he had worried about such things.

The back door bell rang and he went to answer it. The milkman stood there, cashbook in hand, pencil poised.

'Morning, guv, Mrs unwell?'

'No, she's away. How much do I owe you?'

'Two pounds and ten pence, guv.'

He had to go upstairs to get money from his wallet.

'Here you are. How much milk do we usually have?'

The milkman sucked the end of his pencil. 'It varies, but about three pints on average.'

'Then you'd better put me down for one ... Yes, one will be sufficient.'

'Up to you, guv. Daughter away too?'

'What? Yes, she is.'

He thought the man gave him a strange look.

He returned to his breakfast, but somehow the milkman had undermined his newly found confidence. He pushed away the cold toast.

He dressed carefully, putting on his second-best suit, a rough brown tweed which Jean said made him look like a Scottish laird. While he was tying his tie in front of the dressing-table mirror the front door bell rang. He went down.

'Oh, Mrs Lambert—good morning.'

She stood there, the same little twisted smile on her face.

'I can see you've heard, it's all right, isn't it?'

'Yes, it's all right.'

'Like I said, somebody ill?'

'Yes, somebody ill.' He added after a fractional pause, 'Elizabeth has gone with her.' He smiled. 'So I'm on my own for a bit.'

She was staring past him into the hall. 'I'm going into town, so if there's anything I can get...?'

'No, thanks, I have to go anyway.'

'Any little thing I can do....'

'It's very good of you but there really is nothing at the moment.'

He was closing the door ever so slightly and she began to move off.

'Oh, there is one little thing....'

She turned to face him.

'You said that Jean went off in a taxi. Was it a taxi or one of those hire cars?'

Mrs Lambert brightened. 'Well, it was one of those red

taxis, with a light on top—Rubicabs, I think they call them.'

'Thank you.'

'Is that all?'

'Oh, yes.' He smiled. 'I just wondered.'

It had been sunny when he got up, but now it was clouding over and as he closed the door little spots of rain were beginning to fall on the path. He put on his mackintosh and went through the back hall to the garage. When he got out of the car to shut the garage door it was raining hard and he fetched his umbrella.

He drove along the usual route, which was much less busy on Saturday mornings, and when he reached the city centre he turned off down a steep, narrow, concrete ramp to the underground car-park. It was almost deserted and he parked near the exit on the first level.

The pedestrian exit brought him out opposite Jean's office, a five storey Victorian building which had survived the war and post-war development. It was of red brick with little towers at the corners topped by white cupolas. There were shops at ground level, but the rest of the building was occupied by her company and large, cut-out, gilded letters ran right across the street façade: *The Imperial Fire and Life Insurance Society*. He knew that the office was closed on Saturdays and that there was no prospect of finding her there, but he reasoned that she had almost certainly taken the taxi from outside the building, where there was a large rank.

There were five taxis on the rank, of which the first and third were Rubicabs. He went to the third. It was raining so hard that it was barely possible to see through the glass, and he had to tap on the window. The driver wound down the slide.

'Where to?'

He was a young man with a mop of dirty brown hair and two or three days' growth of stubble on his chin.

'I don't want to go anywhere but I wondered if you could help me?' He had to bend down and hold the umbrella away from the cab so that the rain ran down his forehead and face. 'On Friday, about mid-day, one of your cabs took a woman—a youngish woman—from here to—'

26

'It weren't me, mate. I wasn't here on Friday.' He paused. 'Are you the police?'

'No, I ...'

'Then you got no right to be asking questions anyway. Piss off.'

The window was raised and Milton stood, a little shocked, as he always was by gratuitous rudeness. He mopped his face with his handkerchief and moved to the head of the rank.

This time he had to deal with an older man, grey, close-cropped with a bull neck. He was studying the racing page of his newspaper.

'I wonder if you can help me?'

The man was amiable enough, but he had not taken a fare to Barnfield Close on Friday at lunchtime.

'It was a Rubicab.'

'There's fifteen of us chaps on the road, it could have been any one of us.'

After a little more discussion he suggested that the best place to enquire would be the rank at the Midland Station.

'Will you take me there?'

'That's what I'm sitting here for, mister.'

Milton got in and the taxi pulled out into the thin stream of traffic.

'You the police?'

Milton was tempted but he resisted. 'No, I ...'

'I thought not. Private?'

'Yes.'

'You don't look like one of them either. What is it, divorce?'

'Something like that.'

'Well, there's a lot of it about these days.'

There were four Rubicabs in the station yard.

'Here you are, mister, they're all yours and there's thirty-four pence on the clock.'

Milton gave him a pound. 'Keep the change and thanks.'

It had the desired effect. 'I'll have a word if you like. You hang on here and I'll give you a shout if there's any joy. Barnfield Close, midday, yesterday—right?'

'That's right.'

The signal came at the third cab. Milton went over.

'Bert Randall here, he took a lady to Barnfield Close.'

27

Bert Randall was another youngster, but more amenable. 'I waited twenty five minutes for her, then I took her and her luggage to a block of flats in Palmerston Road. What are the new flats by the park called, Jim? Something house....'

'Gladbrook House, is that what you mean?'

'Gladbrook House, that's it. I dropped her there and came back here in time for the 1.30.'

Milton parted with another pound and felt that he had got value for money.

'You want to go there?' his driver enquired. But Milton asked to be taken back to the city centre where he could pick up his own car. The rain had eased to a fine drizzle, but there was no thinning of the clouds which hung over the city, turning morning into dusk.

His success had lifted his spirits; he was pleased with himself.

Palmerston Road lay in the north-west corner of the city, in one of the older suburbs. It struck him as odd that Jean could find her new life within three or four miles of their home. He fetched his car from the underground car-park and drove out there. Palmerston Road ran along one side of Canal Gardens, a public park laid out on the east bank of the old canal. Near the park gates there were a few shops, a church, a bank and a café—the nucleus of some Victorian dream of a garden city. The houses in Palmerston Road were of three or four stories and they had been divided into flats, but on the corner, near the shops, a new block had gone up and a board announced: 'Gladbrook House. High-class, purpose-built flats on long leases. Two to four bedrooms, central heating, communal garden. Sole agents: Stratton and Cove, Palmerston Green. (Near the park gates.)'

Milton left his car by the park railings and crossed the road to the flats. The entrance was austerely impressive. The revolving doors led into a richly carpeted foyer where there were three or four armchairs, two lifts and an illuminated sign-board showing the names of the occupants. Milton studied the sign-board. There were nine floors and a total of thirty five flats, of which about thirty were occupied. None of the names meant anything to him.

'Can I help you, sir?'

A short, stout man in a bottle-green uniform that was too small for him.

'No, I was just looking at your list of tenants.'

'There are a few flats vacant, sir, if you are interested.'

'A lady I know came to live here recently.'

'Perhaps if you told me her name, sir?'

'Oh, the flat wouldn't be in her name.'

The porter was suspicious. 'I think it would be better for you to see the agents, sir. I'm not supposed to discuss the tenants. Stratton and Cove, just across the green, sir.'

He was supervised in his passage through the revolving doors. He had made a mess of that. He crossed to the shops. A baker, a small self-service shop, a hairdresser, a seedy looking café and a chemist. And, of course, the estate agent, Stratton and Cove. He looked at his watch; it was eleven o'clock.

He went into the café, which was empty except for the girl behind the counter. She looked up from the magazine she was reading.

'May I have a cup of coffee, please?'

She served him in silence and he took his coffee to a table by the window.

He could see the entrance to the flats on the other side of the green. His success with the taxi drivers had made it seem easy, but now he was at a loss. He couldn't knock at the doors of thirty flats and ask ... ask what? Unless Jean answered the door to him he would be no further forward.

He saw two or three couples pass through the revolving doors, a man on his own, a young woman with a child. . . . No doubt there was a garage under the flats with direct access to the lifts, so that watching the main entrance was not enough. He would have to think of some other way. It was exasperating sitting there watching the windows, perhaps the window of the very room where Jean was at this moment. From time to time he saw a vague movement in one of the rooms but he was unable to tell whether it was man, woman or child. Then a new idea occurred to him and he was surprised that he had not thought of it before. Surely it was most likely that Jean had met the man at her office—that she worked with him? He felt sure that he was right, and not

29

only did he feel more confident of finding her but the whole thing became somehow less serious. She had not *sought out* another man; they had been thrown together in the course of work. Forty is a dangerous age for a woman.

He got up from his seat by the window, paid for his coffee and, feeling almost jaunty, went two or three doors along the pavement to the estate agent. This time he was prepared.

Behind the window boards with their coloured photographs and beguiling descriptions there was a carpeted office with two desks, one of which was occupied by a sleek young man, all smiles.

'Good morning, sir. How can we help you?'

'I'm interested in the flats in Gladbrook House. I understand that there are some still available?'

'There are still one or two available, sir. That is so.'

'As a matter of fact, I heard about them from a chap I met the other night, a casual acquaintance, who said he lived in one of them.'

'Oh, yes, what was the gentleman's name, sir?'

Milton frowned. 'I've forgotten, though I do remember that he was something to do with insurance.'

The young man's smile broadened. 'That would be Mr Jobling, sir. He has a very nice flat on the second floor, overlooking the park.'

'Jobling? Was that his name? Maybe you're right, it seems to ring a bell. Pleasant sort of chap.'

'Very pleasant. How big a flat do you require, sir? We have them with two, three or four bedrooms.'

'Oh, a small one.'

'Perhaps you would like an order to view?'

'I'd better have some details first so that I can talk it over with my wife.'

'Of course, sir. I'll give you one of our Gladbrook brochures.' He produced a little glossy booklet and handed it over. 'That tells you most things, but if there is anything else you wish to know don't hesitate to get in touch.'

Milton thanked the young man and left. He was elated. He would have Jean back home before the week-end was over. The important thing was that there should be no recriminations. Forgive and forget.

It was raining harder again and he had left his umbrella in the car, but he was scarcely aware of the rain wetting his hair and beginning to trickle down between his neck and his collar. There was more traffic about and he was held up at the broad, triangular intersection which separated him from the flats. By the time he passed once more through the revolving doors his thinning hair was plastered against his scalp and droplets of water ran down his cheeks and nose.

There was no one in the foyer. He glanced at the board. J. K. Jobling: Flat 203. The lift was large and almost silent. He came out on the second floor, a carpeted hall with four doors off and a passage labelled, 'To Emergency Stairs'.

Jobling had a printed card with his name on it inserted in a holder screwed to the door. He pressed the bell and heard it sound distantly in the flat. There was no reply. He tried again, several times, but with no result. He was unreasonably disappointed.

In the foyer he was once more confronted by the porter.

'As you see, I've been to the agent.' He held out the brochure. 'I'm trying to get in touch with Mr Jobling in 203.'

'Mr Jobling's out, sir. He went out early on.'

'Alone?'

The porter seemed reassured by the brochure. 'There was a lady with him.'

'They didn't take the car?'

'No, sir, they were walking.'

It was a set-back, not a defeat.

'I'll call again later.'

It was absurd to feel so let down. He realised that part of his trouble was hunger; he had eaten nothing but a scrap of toast since lunch the previous day. He went back to the café and thought that the young girl behind the counter looked at him with curiosity.

'Do you serve lunches?'

She glanced up at the clock, 'Ten minutes yet.'

'I'll wait. May I have a cup of coffee while I'm waiting?'

She did not answer but started to work the machine. He took his coffee to the same table by the window. The rain was so heavy that it was not easy to see through the glass. After a quarter of an hour the girl brought him a greasy card

31

with the menu written on it in a childish hand.

'There's no steak.'

She was about the same age as Elizabeth but her manner and her expression were those of maturity; she was no longer becoming, she had arrived.

'I'll have the plaice and chips.'

There was little choice, it was that or hamburger and chips. She wiped the table-top with a greasy cloth.

'Bread and butter?'

'No, thank you.'

Two or three other customers came in and settled down with their newspapers. The silence was oppressive. He rubbed an area of window free of condensation with the edge of his hand. The girl called the orders through a hatch to an invisible cook.

He toyed with the fish, which was concealed in an envelope of batter.

'Want a sweet?'

He looked at her enquiringly.

'Fruit salad and cream or ice-cream.'

'I'll have ice-cream, please.'

'Vanilla or strawberry?'

'Vanilla, please.'

It was his only observation point; he had to string out the meal as long as possible. After the ice-cream he ordered a pot of tea. He saw a girlish figure hurrying through the fore-court of the flats to the entrance and for an instant he thought it was Elizabeth, but she turned to look back and he saw that it was an older woman.

At two o'clock the girl stood in front of him with her little bill-pad.

'Coffee, plaice and chips, ice-cream and a pot of tea. That's seventy-five pence.' She put the bill in front of him. 'We close now till half-past three.'

He was the last one in the café and she followed him to the door, switched the notice from 'Open' to 'Closed', and bolted the door behind him.

It was raining as hard as ever, and he could see nowhere to go where he would be sheltered and, at the same time, able to keep the entrance to the flats under observation. He could have gone away and come back later, but he had a feeling amounting to superstition that if he did so he would break the chain of luck which had brought him so far. Unfortunately there was nowhere he could park the car and have a view of the flats.

He walked along the line of shops. The rain was sweeping across the park and driving into doorways. He could feel a cold dampness round his ankles, and it would not be long before the rough tweed of his trousers began to soak up water like a sponge. The shops were built on a slow curve, and at the end of the row there was a sub-branch of one of the banks with a deep doorway that offered some protection. He took up his stand there, hands thrust deep into the pockets of his mackintosh, his wet collar brushing his cheeks.

Activity in the flats seemed to have faded out. Nobody came or went through the revolving doors and there was no sign of movement at any of the windows. He thought he could identify the windows of Jobling's flat, but they were as blank as the rest. The traffic had fallen off too; only an occasional car swished through, throwing up fountains of water.

Where could they have gone—walking in this weather?

At a quarter to three the porter in his green uniform came out through the revolving doors and stood under the canopy, smoking a cigarette.

He was cold and could feel the damp chill stealing up his legs.

It was Saturday afternoon and he tried to reconstruct in his mind a typical wet Saturday afternoon. Jean would probably have washed her hair. She had a set of heated curlers, and if Elizabeth was at home they would have spent some time playing at hairdressing. In any event Jean would have spent much of the afternoon with nothing on but a short bathrobe. In between the various operations she would come into the lounge and sit on the floor, or spread herself in one of the armchairs.

'Don't you think...?'

'Don't I think what?'

'Well, if Elizabeth....'

'My dear man, she knows what I'm like; she's the same herself, or didn't you know?'

33

He would hear them talking in low tones interspersed with giggles. Did they laugh at him?

It was inevitable that if her mother went, Elizabeth would go with her. If he lost one he lost both. He had not seen it so clearly before.

At half past three he went back to the café, where the girl was just drawing the bolts on the door. His mackintosh was covered with dark patches where the water had soaked in.

'You again.' The only non-essential words she had spoken.

He took his coffee to the same table. There was a mirror let into the side of the window and he caught sight of himself in it. What he saw astonished and worried him—he thought he looked like some tramp who had been sleeping rough.

'Is there anywhere I can have a wash and brush-up?'

The girl looked at him before answering. 'There's a toilet at the back.'

But that would mean leaving his post. He was already concerned that twice during the afternoon he had gone down into a little underground convenience near the park entrance.

At five o'clock he had 'tea'—two buns with a film of icing on top and a pot of tea. Because of the rain it was already dusk and the entrance to the flats was lit up. He could see lights in some of the rooms.

In the café customers came and went but most of the time there were only the two of them. The girl stood with her arms resting on the counter, and several times he caught her watching him, but she did not speak.

When it finally happened it was so quick that it was almost over before he realised it. A taxi drew up in the forecourt of the flats, two figures got out, a man and a woman. The man stayed to pay off the cab while the woman ran for the entrance. It was less than fifteen seconds but he was absolutely sure. Jean was wearing her yellow mackintosh which fitted snugly at the waist, and the little waterproof hat to match. But all that was nothing; he would have known that scurrying run anywhere, like a rabbit bolting for cover. The man followed after her as the taxi drove off. He was short, not much taller than Jean, and on the stout side. Milton, who had imagined some slender Adonis, was astounded.

'How much do I owe you?'

'You're not going? We're open till eleven.' She did not smile but he sensed that her sarcasm was good humoured.

He was absurdly excited, but before he left the café he went to the toilet at the back and tried to make himself presentable. There was little he could do with his wet, bedraggled hair and his sodden clothes.

It was still raining when he crossed over to the flats and pushed through the revolving doors. His heart was beating so strongly that his chest seemed to vibrate. The porter, standing in the foyer, looked at him doubtfully.

'They've just gone up, sir.'

'I know.'

'203.'

'I know.'

When he reached the landing he stopped for a moment before ringing the bell. What would he say? To hell with that!

The answer was prompt. The door opened and there was the man he had seen in the forecourt. He had a full, smooth face with pink skin; his hair was dark, turning grey and getting thin.

'I'm Arthur Milton, I've come for my wife.'

The man seemed unperturbed. 'Jean! Your husband is here.'

'I don't want to see him.' The voice came from not far away.

'I want to talk to her.'

'I've told him I'll be in touch in a day or two.'

Jobling looked at Milton, raised his shoulders in a slight shrug and seemed to say, 'There you are, you see how it is.'

'I demand to see her!' Milton was raising his voice.

'Well, I'm not stopping you, Mr Milton, but your wife doesn't want to see you and she's a free agent.'

'She's my wife!' Milton made a move to push Jobling aside.

'Now, don't let's get to that. You know as well as I do that you can't force an entrance if your wife doesn't want to see you.'

Milton was near to despair; it was all turning out so differently. Even the fact that Jobling was a stout, middle-aged man seemed to make matters worse.

'Jean, I want to talk to you!' he shouted.

'No, Arthur.'

35

'I want you to come back to me, Jean.'

'I'm not coming back, Arthur, now or ever, but I will come to see you when we're both calmer—one day next week.'

He knew that he had lost, that it was useless to prolong the agony of this encounter, but he felt driven on by pride or anger or both. He gave Jobling a violent push which sent him reeling across the hall of his flat and confronted Jean, standing just inside the door of one of the rooms. She came towards him.

'Get out! Get out this instant or I'll call the police.' She was so angry that she could barely articulate her words and they came in a harsh, searing whisper. 'Now!'

He went, and on the landing he met the porter, who turned his back and pretended to be doing something with the fire hose locker. The door of the flat slammed shut.

He had wandered half way up Palmerston Road before he remembered his car. He went back, got in the car, and sat there for a long time staring at the windscreen, which was carrying so much water that nothing could be seen through it. In the end he started the car and drove off.

He lost himself twice and on one occasion pulled up outside a pub in an empty street. He got out of his car and went in. There were not many in the bar and his arrival drew attention. His clothes dripped on the tiled floor.

'I want a bottle of brandy.' He added, after a moment, 'To take away.'

The barman gave him a queer look and Milton was aware of muffled laughter behind him.

'What sort of brandy, sir?' He reeled off three or four brand names.

'Any sort.'

He was surprised at what it cost and his surprise showed.

'Would you prefer a half-bottle, sir?'

'No, no, this will do,' and he went out with the unwrapped bottle under his arm.

He knew that they would burst out laughing when he closed the door, but why was he so ridiculous?

He reached home at last and put the car away. He barely had time to switch on the kitchen light when the front door bell rang. He answered it. Mrs Lambert was standing there in the darkness, an umbrella over her head.

'I heard you come in. Elizabeth was here....'

'When?'

'She came twice: this morning about eleven and again this evening, about six or half past. She collected some of her things but she wanted to see you.'

Milton was staring at her blankly, and the woman did not know what to say next. In the end he shut the door in her face. Elizabeth had been here, waiting for him, while he was degrading himself at the flat.

He went back to the kitchen. Propped against the bread board was a folded piece of paper. He opened and read it:

Dear Daddy,
I'm sorry, truly sorry,
Elizabeth

Chapter Three

THAT NIGHT THE brandy was not so effective. He dozed fitfully, disturbed by vague, rather frightening dreams, and when he finally woke in the morning he had a hangover.

His appearance when he looked in the bathroom mirror shocked him. He had aged; his cheeks were hollow, and his eyes seemed to have retreated into their sockets.

'I must take a grip on myself.'

He had a bath and shaved carefully, then he spread out his wet tweed suit on a sort of towel-rail in the airing closet. His mackintosh, still dripping, he suspended over the bath.

Downstairs it depressed him to see the fragments of toast, the dirty cup and saucer and the butter still in its paper wrapper as he had left it the morning before. He went out to collect the pint of milk which stood by the dustbin. It would be a good idea to have a proper breakfast, but an egg would be too cloying. In one of the cupboards he found several packets of cereals. He chose one, tipped some into a dish, and added milk and sugar. He could cope with that. It was nine o'clock and the day stretched ahead of him like a vast, featureless desert.

He usually got up before Jean on Sunday mornings, though he did no more than make a cup of tea. She would come down and find him sitting in the kitchen, drinking tea and reading the Sunday paper. He took the *Observer*, Jean had the *Express*. This morning both papers lay on the mat by the front door.

'I must get organised.'

Although his head ached he forced himself to make plans. There was no fresh food in the house so today he would make do with tins, but tomorrow he would go shopping on his way home from school. He started going through the cupboards systematically with a shopping list on the table. At lunchtime he boiled some potatoes and ate them with a few slices of tinned meat. After lunch he washed up and tidied the kitchen; then he made a pot of tea and took it into his study, where there was a pile of marking waiting to be done. Slowly, dimly, he was beginning to see the possibility of a new routine. '... *You'll soon get over it once you've got a new routine.*' He didn't believe that, but he was determined not to go under.

He worked conscientiously through thirty-one fourth-form exercises, writing neat comments in the margins and awarding to each a grade which he entered in his record book. Then he started on sixth-form essays—'British Sea Power in the Napoleonic Wars'. After reading three of the essays he gave up and began to wander round the house. He went upstairs with no conscious purpose. The landing was dimly lit through a pair of lancet windows with coloured glass, and he stood there for some time looking at the five closed doors and feeling that he was about to do something improper, even shameful. He opened the door of Elizabeth's room and went in. He could not remember how long it was since the last time he had been in her room—certainly not since it was redecorated three or four years ago.

The room was cold and lifeless. A square, unfaded patch on the bench which formed part of a built-in unit, showed where her record player had stood. There were still books on the shelves and posters on the walls, a new generation of posters in shades of green and blue and mauve, vague unisex figures reminiscent of Beardsley and mildly suggestive. The divan was covered with a striped linen bed-spread which picked up the turquoise colour in the carpet. Whose taste? He had no idea. Probably it was the result of one of those seemingly endless discussions between mother and daughter, discussions which were broken off as soon as he came into the room.

He slid back the door of the wardrobe. Summer dresses on hangers, a pair of blue slacks and a school mack obviously too small. On the floor, a few pairs of shoes and sandals and in one corner, a one-eyed teddy bear he had forgotten.

He looked at the books on the shelves, a mixed bag. D. H. Lawrence rubbed shoulders with Brian Aldiss and Queneau; Harold Robbins with Jean Paul Sartre and Ian Fleming. He took down a book at random and a sheet of notepaper, folded in half, fluttered to the floor.

Dearest Liz,

I'm missing you. If I must be honest I'm counting the days. I know I said I didn't want to come but that wasn't true, it's just that I couldn't ask mother for the money as things are. You seem to be enjoying France but don't start getting ideas about sexy Frenchmen or there will be an international incident.

I managed to translate your story about the chimpanzees but I had to guess two words which weren't in the dictionary. Now I can't help giggling every time I think of it and mother thinks I'm round the twist.

Getting back to sexy Frenchmen I think you should wear a label, like the Yanks—I belong to A. W. Just so's there's no misunderstanding.

Until you come home here's a big kiss to be going on with—X. There are plenty more where that came from but they will be delivered personally.

I love you—would you believe?

I do, anyway,

6 days 17 hours from now....

Alan

Elizabeth had gone to France with a school party during the summer holidays.

He stood holding the letter for a long time, then he folded it and slipped it into his wallet.

There were several drawers in the unit and he opened the top one. It held handkerchiefs, an old handbag and four or five cosmetic bottles and jars. The second drawer was empty except for a brassière with broken elastic. He picked it up shyly, held it for a moment, then placed it against his cheek.

Next morning he was up early and he was in the kitchen eating his cornflakes when the cleaning-woman came. She arrived at the back door, which was not unlocked, and he had to let her in.

'I had a note from your wife saying to come early before you was off to school. She seemed to think you'd be wanting me to put in more time.'

Milton, caught on the hop, had no idea what to say.

'What happened, then? Gone off and left you has she?'

'I shall be on my own from now on.'

She looked round the kitchen disparagingly. 'I'm not surprised, I seen it coming. Anyway, I'll help if I can. Walking out like that! Some don't know when they're well off. Daughter gone too?'

Milton felt the tension rising. He was gripping the edge of the table.

'What do I owe you, Mrs Watson?'

'Owe me? You don't owe me nothing till Friday.'

'I mean in lieu of notice.'

'Notice? Is that how it is? I can find other work, don't you fret, but I'm entitled to a week....'

'How much?'

'I get eight pound.'

He took out his wallet and counted out the notes.

She went out of the door, looking back at him, unable to believe what had happened.

He drove to school as usual and parked his car. He did not have a form to supervise, so he was accustomed to spending the half-hour devoted to registration and assembly in laying out his work for the day—notes, slides, a film if he was going to use one, maps and charts which he had collected over the years. But this morning, before starting on any of that, he went along to the room where Elizabeth registered with her group and peered through the glass panel in the door. He could not see her among the young people milling about but at that moment Tom Reid, their form master, caught his eye and opened the door.

'Hullo, Arthur, looking for me? I see Liz isn't here this morning....'

Tom called all his flock by diminutives. Milton thought quickly.

'No, that's what I came to tell you. She's not very well.'

'Oh, I'm sorry about that. Give her our love and tell her we hope she'll be better soon.'

'Yes, yes, I will.'

His classes went badly. Before break he had a confrontation with a boy in the fifth and was put in a false and humiliating

41

situation. It was the last period of the morning when he had his upper-sixth history set which included Alan Wilson. They seemed to sense his uneasiness and respond to it by being restless themselves. He lost his temper once or twice and several times he caught himself staring at the Wilson boy, who would flush and look away.

Just before afternoon school was due to begin Milton went to the school office.

'I would like the address of Alan Wilson in the sixth. He came to us at the beginning of last term and he's in Tom Reid's group.'

'His address?' The girl who looked after records was surprised; it was unusual for a master not concerned with administration to ask for pupils' addresses.

'That's what I said.'

'My! We are sharp today.'

She went to a filing cabinet and took out a buff envelope. 'Here you are, that's all we've got on him.'

He slid the papers out on her desk. 'You don't mind?'

'Be my guest but hurry up, I've got work to do.'

His record card from his previous school, a recommendation from the headmaster and an admission slip signed by his mother. He made a note of the address: Flat 5G, Farley House, Gordon Street. It was not far from the school.

'She's a widow, her husband died three months ago. That's why they moved. They're with relatives in Gordon Street.'

'You've seen her?'

'She came in with the boy to see the head before he started here.'

'What sort of woman is she?'

He got an odd look. 'What's the attraction? Thinking of trying your luck? She's a bit old for you—all of fifty-five, I should think—but still blonde, though now it comes from a bottle.'

Milton felt that he had to make some explanation. 'I'm interested because he's a candidate for Oxford.'

'Good for him, but does mum have to qualify too?'

On his way home from school he drove down Gordon Street. On one side there were terraced houses with little front gardens but on the other, developers had put up blocks of flats.

'Flats for the lower and middle income range' was probably how estate agents would classify them.

On Tuesday morning there were two envelopes on the mat. One was a bill for the telephone, the other was addressed to him in Jean's writing. He tore it open. It covered two pages of thick white notepaper headed with the Gladbrook address.

I'm sorry that you were so upset on Saturday but it was your own fault. You will have to accept the fact that I have gone for good. We shall have to meet because there are arrangements to be made but it will be of no use unless you are prepared to talk reasonably.

I'm asking for nothing. The house and everything in it is yours. I shall be well provided for and so will Elizabeth if she chooses to stay with us.

I wrote to Mrs Watson and I hope she agreed to put in more hours to look after you properly. I kept Elizabeth home from school because, after Saturday, I didn't want her to be upset by a scene at school. I will come along to the house on Tuesday evening about seven unless you phone me at work to say otherwise. I hope we shall be able to part sensibly and that Elizabeth will be able to go back to school on Wednesday without having to face a crisis. I know I've treated you badly but that's life. People do hurt each other and sometimes those who least deserve it are hurt most.

Jean

He read the letter standing by the front door, then he put it back in its envelope and into his pocket. He could feel the smart of tears in his eyes, mainly because of the phrase, 'I hope we shall be able to part sensibly'.

That evening he got home early from school and spent some time tidying the house. He had brought home a bottle of sherry.

Though painful, the interview with Jean was not as humiliating as he had feared. She complimented him on the way the house was kept.

'Mrs Watson must be looking after you very well.'

'She doesn't come any more.'

'Doesn't come?'

'I stopped her.'

43

'But you. . . .' She broke off, realising that she now had no right to interfere.

He offered her sherry and she accepted.

'My, but you're breaking out, Arthur!'

Then she came to the point. 'I want a divorce, Arthur. Ken wants to marry me.'

'And do you want to marry him?'

She gave a nervous laugh. 'I'm not bothered one way or the other but he wants to make an honest woman of me.'

'Are you asking me to provide grounds?'

She looked surprised. 'Good God, no, Arthur! I'm not that bad. In any case it wouldn't do you any good at school. No, I want you to divorce me.'

She looked away as she spoke.

'If that's what you want.'

'It's very good of you, Arthur. I know you'll hate every minute of it.'

'I'll miss you, Jean.'

It was obvious that she was moved. 'Yes, I know.'

'It isn't just a question of finding a new routine.'

'No.'

'I want to maintain Elizabeth. I mean, I want to provide for her.'

'Even if she lives with me?'

'It doesn't matter where she lives.'

'I'll tell her.'

'There's no need.'

'I think she should know.'

He saw her to the door. 'Did you come by bus?'

'Yes.' She looked at him quickly then added, 'No, that's a lie. Ken is waiting for me in the car round the corner.'

'I'll make an appointment with the solicitor as soon as I can.'

'Thanks, it's more than I've any right to ask.'

She was wearing her coffee-coloured coat with the fur trimmings and she looked like a young girl as she hurried across the road and turned the corner out of sight.

Mrs Lambert would be watching from one of her windows.

He closed the front door and stood there for a moment. He seemed to be quivering all over, as though every nerve was exposed. Then he went slowly through to his study and sat at his desk. He took out his keys and unlocked one of the drawers, lifted out several large envelopes labelled 'Insurance', 'Car', 'Income Tax'. From under them all he took out a smaller, grey envelope which contained some letters and a single photograph. It was a postcard-sized photograph of a young girl with fair, wavy hair. She was smiling shyly at the camera, her head tilted slightly to one side. 'From Christine with love, June 1956.'

The resemblance to the boy, Wilson, was uncanny.

Elizabeth returned to school on the day after Jean's visit. Their first encounter was a chance one in the corridor. She smiled and walked on. That evening she was sitting in the car when he went to collect it from the car-park. It gave him a shock to see her there, as though time had slipped.

'You don't mind? I wanted to see you.'

'Of course I don't mind!'

He wanted to take her in his arms and hold her, but he had been unable to allow himself any physical contact with her since she was eight or nine. He blamed Jean's capacity for cheerfully obscene innuendo. A peck on the cheek at bed-time and in the morning.

'I'll take you home.'

He saw by her expression that she had misunderstood.

'To the flat.'

He started the car and drove out of the car-park.

'I'd like to come and see you one evening, daddy.'

He was holding the steering wheel with both hands, looking straight ahead.

'You don't want to come back to live? Be truthful, Elizabeth.'

'No, you know that I've always got on so well with mummy. That doesn't mean that. . . .'

'No, of course not.'

'How do you get on with . . .' he hesitated, '. . . with Ken?'

'All right. He's very nice to me.'

'I don't think it would be a very good idea for you to come to the house. Let us meet like this some nights. Let me take you home now and then instead of going by bus.' He waited. 'You understand?'

'I think so,' and after a moment she added, 'yes, I do.' She put her hand over his.

He dropped her by the park gates and watched her scurry across the road and into the flats. Just like her mother. She waved from the revolving doors.

On the surface he seemed to carry on much as usual: he taught his classes, marked their work and attended the first practice for *A Child of Our Time*. The news of his break with Jean filtered through his circle of acquaintances and as it did so their attitudes towards him changed. They went out of their way to be pleasant, and one or two ventured on sympathy. But he had changed both mentally and physically. He had lost weight, his features had fined down and his eyes were restless—wary, like a rabbit caught out in the open. He became even more taciturn and when spoken to he sometimes found it difficult to turn his thoughts from some inner preoccupation.

On the Friday of the second week after Jean left him, Bates, the headmaster, stopped him in the corridor.

'Are you free at all today, Arthur?'

'The period after break.'

'Perhaps you will come to my room for a word?'

Bates had started as a careerist, full steam ahead for the top, but at thirty-five he had achieved his present headship and he had never quite made up his mind where he wanted to go after that. Now, at forty-six, he accepted the fact that he was unlikely to go anywhere and his energy dissipated itself more or less harmlessly in sporadic programmes of reorganisation. All the same, his manner was still that of a devotee of what Mr Polly called 'The Shovacious Cult'.

'Sit down, Arthur, just a word. . . .'

The telephone rang and Bates answered it. 'No, Gwenda, don't put him through, say I'll ring him back. And Gwenda—keep me clear of calls and interruptions for the next fifteen minutes, please.'

Which meant that the word must be serious.

He turned to Milton, smiling. 'There, at least we shall be undisturbed.'

He had reddish hair and a clipped, bristly moustache which gave him a military air.

'This morning, just after assembly, I had a visit from Alan Wilson, the boy who came into the sixth last term. He had already spoken to Jim Wiles, his year tutor, who referred him to me.'

Milton looked mildly receptive.

The headmaster fiddled with his blotter. 'He wants to give up history.' Bates said it with a nervous giggle as though telling a joke in bad taste.

Milton said nothing.

'Do you know why he wants to give it up?'

'Me? No, but I imagine that you asked him that.'

Another little laugh, 'I did, as a matter of fact. Do you know what he said?'

'How could I?'

Milton had never been very good at playing the headmaster's verbal games.

'He said that it was because of you; he said that you treated him differently from the others in the set.' Bates looked at him, inviting him to expose the absurdity of such a statement.

'He's probably right.'

An incredulous wave of the hand.

'No, I mean it. For some reason I don't get on with the boy and, of course, he doesn't get on with me.'

'A rather serious situation for a boy intending to read history at university, isn't it?'

'Yes.'

Bates was puzzled by Milton's attitude: detached, objective, almost indifferent.

'Of course one has to recognize such clashes of personality, especially in sixth-form teaching.'

'Yes.'

'It seems a great pity for him to give up history though, don't you think?'

'Yes.'

It was as though he were completing a verbal questionnaire.

Bates looked at him for some time before speaking again. 'I wondered if you could make any suggestion, Arthur?'

'I don't think I can.'

47

'How would you view the possibility of putting him with young Collins for say, three or four tutorial periods a week? Collins is lightly time-tabled this term.'

Collins was the latest addition to the staff of Milton's department.

'If Collins will take him.'

'Oh, I'm sure he will; it will be a good chance for him to get his teeth into some sixth-form work.'

'Yes. I'll arrange it. Is that all?'

Milton stood up, Bates did not.

'I heard about you and Jean ... I'm very sorry, such a very great pity.'

'Yes.'

'No possibility... ?'

'None.'

'And Elizabeth?'

'She will continue at school.'

'Of course, my dear fellow, I wasn't prying.' He paused, playing with his fountain pen. 'You are not well, Arthur, anybody can see that.'

'Is my work unsatisfactory?'

Bates swivelled in his chair. 'My dear chap! How can you... ? Damn it all, after all these years, Arthur, I look upon our relationship as one of friendship. One wants to help.'

'Thank you, but I shall sort out my problems.'

'I'm quite sure that you will, quite sure. However, even the strongest of us sometimes needs help.'

'What kind of help do you think I need—psychiatric?'

'You were always one for dotting the "i"s and crossing the "t"s, Arthur. I merely thought that in circumstances like yours one might benefit from a little....'

'Support?'

Bates laughed in a strained way. 'I know that's almost a dirty word these days but in the best sense, I suppose that is what I do mean.'

'As you say, in the best sense. I must go, I have a little preparation to do.'

'Do think over what I've said, Arthur.'

'Of course.'

He felt angered and humiliated by the interview, though he realised that he had brought it on himself.

He went to the history prep-room, where they stored books and equipment. Collins was there duplicating test papers. Collins was twenty-five, poised and immaculate. He wore glasses with oblong lenses in thin gold frames.

'Have you seen him?'

'Have I seen who?' Milton looked vague.

'The head.'

'I've just left him.'

'What about it, then? Am I to take over Wilson?'

Milton stared at him but said nothing.

He was teaching himself to cook, and tonight was his second night on a beef-stew he had prepared. All he had to do was to heat it and let it simmer for a while. After his meal he washed up. He could not bear the thought of dirty dishes in the sink; they seemed to menace him. At half past seven he had finished his marking and was trying to make up his mind whether or not to call on the Wilsons. Indoors he felt safe, in command of the situation; he even hated to have people coming to the door, and when they did he would not let them in. But he wanted to see where the boy lived and to speak to his mother. Finally he made up his mind to go.

He got out the car and drove to Gordon Street. It was a foggy evening with drizzling rain and most of the flats had their curtains drawn and lights on. Flat 5G had a yellow door and an illuminated bell-push. As he rang he could hear the sound of a radio or television coming from inside, but after a second ring the door was opened by a tall, angular woman with pale, haggard features and bleached, lifeless hair. She wore a maroon woollen dress which was draped from her shoulders as though from a hanger.

'Mrs Wilson?'

She had difficulty with her breathing and paused between every two or three words. 'No, I'm her sister. She's here if you want her ... Jane! there's somebody to see you.'

Alan's mother certainly looked younger, plumper and healthier than her sister and she retained something of the good looks which had been hers as a girl.

'My name is Milton, I teach Alan at school.'

She was a pleasant soul and seemed overawed by a visit from her son's teacher. She took him into the living room; a middle-aged man in shirt sleeves came out as they went in. She switched off the television.

'I'm sorry, I seem to be turning everybody out.'

'Don't worry about that. Is Alan in some sort of trouble?'

'No, on the contrary, he is doing very well.'

'He's not in at the moment; he takes his books to the public library and works there because of the television. Joyce —that's my sister—likes it on and as she's a very sick woman. . . .' She smoothed the green chenille tablecloth with a small and surprisingly delicate hand. Milton watched her hand, fascinated.

'You wanted to talk to me about Alan?'

'Yes. I don't know if he's told you that he will be sitting his Oxford entrance examination soon now.'

She smiled. 'Yes, he told me. I don't understand these things, I just want what is best for him. He's a good boy, never a minute's trouble, a real comfort.'

'Yes, I'm sure he is.'

She went to the window to straighten the curtains. 'He's just lost his father; I don't expect he told you. That's why we moved back here really. His father had a good job on the railway—a foreman. Fifty-eight, he was—went off just like that, no warning, nothing. Heart it was. I had no idea.' She blinked rapidly over her tears.

'I'm very sorry.'

'Yes, we're a family that's had more than its share of troubles. Now there's Joyce. . . .' The little white hand smoothed the tablecloth incessantly. 'So it seemed the best thing to move in here. Joyce is too ill to look after the flat and her husband. I suppose you could say it's worked out.'

She twisted the wedding-ring on her finger. Her complexion as a girl must have been pink and white like her son's. Now she had a high colour, and the skin of her neck and chest in the V-neck of her blouse was blotchy.

'You've lived here before?'

'Oh, yes. Jim and me both came from these parts—Jim was my husband. When we got married we went to live in

50

Bewdley Street and we lived there, in the same house, for thirty years—until Alan was ten. We only moved then because Jim was offered this promotion if we moved to Bristol.'

There was a framed photograph over the fireplace, an enlargement of one similar to the postcard he had in the grey envelope in his desk. Wherever he looked, his eyes kept coming back to the photograph, and she noticed.

'I expect you can see the likeness.'

He tried to look blank.

'To Alan—that's Christine, his sister. She was the same age then as he is now.' She took to smoothing the tablecloth again and after a little while she added, 'We lost her, that same year the photograph was taken.'

'I'm sorry.'

'I sometimes think Alan was sent to take her place; I was forty-one when he was born and we'd given up the idea that we might....'

There were questions he could have asked, easily and naturally but he remained silent.

'Would you like a cup of something, Mr Milton?'

'No, thank you. I must be getting along.' He stood up.

'It was nice of you to come to see us—to show interest. I know the school will do what's right for him.'

She did not seem to think there was anything odd about his visit; it did not occur to her to wonder why he had come. She saw him to the door and waited with him for the lift to arrive.

'Good night, Mrs Wilson.'

Mother and daughter. Mother and son.

Why had he gone? He was not clear in his mind, but he knew that it was part of a growing need to placate, to appease and above all, to know.

He drove slowly home.

It was odd, the feeling of relief which he experienced as he closed the front door for the night. Almost as though he had once more successfully evaded pursuit. The house was becoming his refuge. He rarely opened any windows, and the curtains were drawn back just far enough to avoid comment. At the approach of darkness he closed them completely and it was only then that he felt truly secure.

51

Chapter Four

ON FRIDAY EVENING he went to see his doctor. It was Guy Fawkes night, a typical November evening, chilly and damp.

'Not sleeping?'

The doctor looked into his eyes, pulled down the lids, felt round his neck and looked into his ears.

'Any particular reason?'

'I suppose I've had a rather worrying time recently.'

'You're a school teacher, aren't you?'

'It's nothing to do with my job.'

'You'd better let me examine you—on the couch.'

Cold, hard fingers prodded and explored; he was sounded, he had his blood-pressure taken and his reflexes tested.

'Appetite all right? ... Bowels? ... Waterworks? ... All right you can dress now.'

Back at his desk, pen poised over prescription pad: 'This worrying time you've been having—domestic problems?'

'My wife has left me.'

'Ah!'

Milton thought: 'Now he thinks he's reached the core of the problem. No need to look any further; a few tablets....'

'I'll give you something to make you sleep. Don't take too many, two should be enough.'

The doctor scribbled briefly. From somewhere in the house there came a dull thud followed by the sound of a child crying. Then a woman's voice: 'There, now! What did mummy tell you? If you're not a good boy mummy won't take you to see the lovely bonfire.'

The doctor looked up with a faint smile, in which there was an element of the conspiratorial.

'Any hobbies?'

'I sing with the local choral society.'

'Try to get out more. A brisk walk before bed is a good thing.' He handed over the prescription.

Milton stood up. 'Thanks.'

'Come again in a fortnight—sooner if you want to. There's nothing organically wrong with you.'

He was out on the pavement with the prescription in his pocket. Rockets shot up sporadically, each exploding in a shower of stars and a faint plop. At the end of the road, on a piece of waste ground, a bonfire had just been lit. He could smell the smoke, mixed with paraffin, as the flames licked up the pyramid to the guy at the top. Adults and children formed a ring at a respectful distance and within the circle somebody was letting off more fireworks; catherine wheels, Roman candles and fountains of golden rain. He stood watching for a while, tall enough to see over the crowd. One or two adults turned to look at him, a middle-aged man on his own. He felt uncomfortable and walked on.

He did not want to return home just yet. If the doctor had spent more time with him and asked questions, would it have helped?

'I feel afraid most of the time.'

'What are you afraid of?'

'I don't know.'

'Are you very much in love with your wife?'

'No, I don't think so.'

'Are there any children?'

'I have a daughter who is nearly seventeen; she left with her mother.'

'Are you fond of her?'

'Yes.'

'If they came back—?'

'I don't want them back.'

'Then what's it all about?'

'I don't know.'

Even when he asked himself the questions the answers came out wrong. Of course he loved his wife, of course he wanted her back. . . .

He walked at random through the dark streets and next time he became aware of his surroundings he was in a poorer locality, a street of little red-brick houses with tiny front gardens from which the railings had been removed. There was a pub on the corner and he went in. He felt the need to renew contact, to put himself in the context of other human beings.

The pub was busy. One group played darts, some sat at tables, others pressed round the bar, where two men were serving. The clock over the bar showed a quarter to nine. They made way for him, a stranger, an oddity. A fat man with sweat running down his face took his order.

'One medium sherry coming up.'

'Evening Mr Milton.'

The other barman was a youth with shoulder-length hair and a thin, foxy face. Milton had once tried to teach him history.

'Bottrell, isn't it?'

'The one and only; refuse all substitutes. Having a night on the town, Mr Milton?'

Milton retreated from the bar, gulped down his sherry and left.

It was raining harder and he turned up the collar of his raincoat.

For twenty years he had rigorously schooled himself in a particular rôle; he had contrived for himself an image which he presented to the world at large, and so faithfully had he lived up to that image that he had seemed to become what he represented himself to be. The past had been obliterated or, at least, securely tucked away in the Pandora's box of his unconscious. Now the whole edifice of his contrivance seemed to be threatened.

Because his wife and daughter had left him?

'What are you afraid of?'

'I'm not sure.'

A name-plate on a house wall read Bewdley Street. He knew where he was now, and he could scarcely believe that chance had brought him there. Bewdley Street. And Bewdley Street led into Commercial Road. If he turned up Commercial Road he would be in Palmerston Green, at the flats.

Was it a sign? A warning?

He shivered and quickened his pace.

Commercial Road was poorly lit and deserted. On one side

54

the canal ran in a deep cutting; on the other, former warehouses were now used by builders' merchants, scrap dealers
and cash-and-carry traders of every description. A police
patrol car coming towards him slowed down and he was aware
of the driver's scrutiny.

He crossed the bridge over the canal and reached the green.
The shops were in darkness except for the café, where an
orange glow showed dimly through the steamy windows. On
the other side of the junction the foyer of Gladbrook House
was brilliantly lit, but the windows of the flats showed few
lights. In one of the rooms Elizabeth would be doing her
homework, reading or listening to records; in another Jean
would be sitting on the floor watching television and wearing
only a dressing gown which persistently fell away from her
thighs.

Then he remembered that it was Friday and on Friday
evenings Elizabeth sometimes went to a pottery class at the
institute. The class was over at nine, so if she had gone she
would soon be back. He was overcome by a feeling of tenderness and by a longing to see and speak to her. He crossed to
the bus-stop on the corner and waited in the shelter of a
doorway. A few minutes later a double-decker drew up briefly.
Nobody got off or on, the conductor rang his bell and the
bus moved off. He decided to wait for the next one.

There were few people about; a man went by, walking his
dog, a policeman strolled past, a couple with their arms round
each other, regardless of the drizzling rain . . . They had passed
him before he realised that the girl was Elizabeth and the
boy, Alan Wilson. They stopped only a few feet away. She
was looking up at the boy, clinging to him. They were close
enough for Milton to see the moisture glistening on her parted
lips. The boy bent his head and kissed her lips very gently,
but she clasped her hands behind his neck and arched her
body against him, turning his caress into a passionate em-
brace. They remained together for some time, then she broke
free and they crossed the intersection hand-in-hand. At the
entrance to the flats they parted. She stood in the light, looking after him and he turned to wave twice before an angle
in the buildings cut off their view of each other.

Milton remained where he was long after Elizabeth had

gone in. He felt drained of all feeling, numbed. He walked slowly past the shops to the café, pushed open the door and went in. All the tables were occupied, mostly men in shabby raincoats. This was evidently one of the times when the place came into its own. Each of the men had a newspaper propped in front of him and the remnants of a meal. The only sound came from the gurgling of the coffee machine. The girl waitress was perched on her stool behind the counter, her arms folded on the plastic top.

She was not much older than Elizabeth and she would have been pretty if her expression had been less sullen.

'You again.'

Her manner was not unfriendly: faintly amused, a little contemptuous.

'May I have a cup of coffee, please?'

She smiled and her face was transformed. It was obvious that she thought him comic, but why? What had he said or done?

He took his coffee to a table where there was a man who looked rather less down-and-out than the others and pulled out a chair.

'You don't mind?'

The man looked up but did not answer. Everything about the place was tatty, even squalid. A torpid fly crawled among the crumbs on his table and investigated the glutinous mess round the neck of the sauce bottle. The smell of the place blended stale cooking fat with cigarette smoke, wet clothing and coffee. A wretched little café, yet the total effect had an unreal, nightmarish quality like something out of Kafka. He had been there some time before he looked up at the clock, which advertised a brand of soft drinks, and saw that it was a quarter past ten.

The next day was Saturday and he had planned the weekend with care, leaving as little idle time as possible. He got up at eight, bathed and dressed and went downstairs. He ate a boiled egg with two pieces of bread and butter and drank two cups of coffee. At ten o'clock he drove into town to do his shopping. It was another grey day with louring clouds and frequent showers. He parked in the city centre and went to a supermarket which was linked to the car-park by a covered way so that he could bring his purchases to the car in the little trolley.

'Now for the library!'

By talking to himself in this way he created the illusion that he was busy, with all sorts of interesting things waiting to be done. In fact, one of his sixth form pupils was working on a project about the development of communications between 1740 and 1840 and in order to assess it fairly there were points he needed to look up.

The city library was part of a large neo-Gothic building, the City Art Gallery and Museum, a gift of some long dead philanthropist who believed that the millennium might be hastened by bringing culture within reach of the labouring classes.

Milton spent a couple of hours in the great vaulted reference library, reading about stage-coaches, semaphore telegraphs, nascent railways and steam-ships. When he had finished he put the last book back on the shelves with regret. The morning had recalled his student days when he had a clearly defined objective and he was under continuous pressure to achieve it. Now, of course, there was nothing to stop him from undertaking a study project or even a piece of historical research, but it would not be the same; there would be no sense of urgency and he knew that he would soon begin to see his efforts as futile against the broader background of his life.

As he walked down the long room towards the exit his attention was caught by a bay labelled 'Psychology'. On an impulse, and with the air of a man entering a pornographic book-shop, he went into the bay and picked up a book at random. He turned to the index and glanced down the columns until he came to the word 'Guilt'. He looked up the first of the page references and read a few lines:

'A feeling of guilt may be responsible for greater tension than was relieved by the act which gave rise to it. Many people cannot control their sense of guilt and punish themselves disproportionately for trivial offences....'

But what if the offence was not trivial?

He tried two other books but found no mention of guilt. What sort of psychology can ignore it? However, in the fourth book he found something more:

'... The unsatisfied tension of inwardly directed mortido arising from "wickedness" shows itself as a need for punishment ... *Until this need for punishment is satisfied, it will continue to exist, and quantities of this tension may build up for years eventually driving the individual into scrape after scrape in order to obtain relief.*'

He closed the book quickly and returned it to the shelves, then he hurried through the swing doors and down the steps into watery sunshine. He felt as though he had come back from a journey and had to accustom himself once more to normal surroundings.

The body was found by a man exercising his dog on the tow-path. It lay, face downwards, in the ditch between the towpath and the massive stone-wall of the cutting. The man telephoned Central Police Station. Detective Sergeant Hammond and Detective Constable Symons were first on the scene.

Hammond was short for a policeman; he wore a shabby raincoat and a cloth cap; he had a thin, sad face with small, bright eyes. A disillusioned terrier. His companion was young, good looking and inclined to be dim.

The body rested on a cushion of brambles which choked the ditch. Hammond eyed it with disfavour because it was going to spoil his Saturday.

'He must have been here all night.'

The dead man was short and tubby; his clothes were sodden from the rain but they seemed to be of good quality. A light-weight raincoat, grey, worsted trousers with a fine purple stripe, grey suède shoes and silk socks to match. His head was bare and his thinning hair was dark. His right temple had been smashed in by a powerful blow and was crusted with blood.

Hammond looked up at the parapet twenty feet above him.

'It looks as though he was clobbered in Commercial Road and pushed over.'

For the traders of Commercial Road, Saturday was a bonanza, with business overflowing into the street and stopping the traffic. Few people had the curiosity to look over the wall to see what was happening on the tow-path below.

Detective Chief Superintendent Goddard arrived with the police surgeon and a photographer. They were closely followed by two men with a stretcher.

'We shall have to get him up the steps, sir; it's going to be awkward.'

Their work was hampered by a heavy shower but at last the body had been photographed from every possible angle and lifted on the stretcher.

The dead man must have been in his forties. He was obviously prosperous and accustomed to doing himself well; he was overweight and his full, rather fleshy features would almost certainly have carried a high colour in life.

Hammond, searching about in the ditch below where the body had been, came up with a pig-skin wallet. Goddard took it from him and looked at the contents: forty pounds in notes, a credit card and driving licence and a few stamps. The card and licence had been issued to Kenneth John Jobling, Flat 203, Gladbrook House, Palmerston Green.

Goddard handed the wallet back to Hammond. 'I'll leave that to you.'

Milton treated himself to lunch in a restaurant which specialised in French food, but afterwards he could not have said what he had eaten. He had intended to spend the afternoon cleaning the house, but the heart had gone out of him and he turned into the first cinema he came to.

He seemed to be losing contact, a little more each day. It was as though he no longer belonged to the same world as the people who jostled him in the street or those who stood up for him to pass along the row in the cinema. He was being separated from them by events of which he had no clear recollection, no more than a series of pictures which came to him in an unintelligible sequence.

The film must have been in the X-category for as his eyes became accustomed to the dim light he saw that the audience was mostly male and on the screen nude bodies writhed and contorted themselves. How absurd it all was—as though the whole world was contained between a woman's thighs.

The film ended. There was an interval, then another film,

but he must have fallen asleep for he had no idea what it was about.

At five o'clock he came out into the cold grey light of an autumn afternoon. For a moment he was not sure where he was, then he got his bearings and set off in the direction of the car-park. By the entrance a newsvendor sat on a stool, a pile of papers beside him. A bill-board against the wall had been scrawled over with a felt pen:

FATAL MUGGING IN COMMERCIAL ROAD

It was the road which caught his eye and he bought a paper. The front page stories were about other things but he found the item tucked away in the late news:

FATAL MUGGING

News has just come in of the discovery of a body on the canal tow-path in Commercial Road. The dead man is believed to be Mr K. J. Jobling, a well known insurance consultant. It is thought that Mr Jobling was attacked in Commercial Road and that his body was subsequently pushed over the parapet into the ditch which runs by the tow-path.

The investigation is under the direction of Detective Chief Superintendent Goddard, head of C.I.D.

'You ain't helping my trade, mate, standing there.'

He was standing directly in front of the paper seller.

'Sorry.'

He folded his newspaper and went to fetch his car. He was reluctant to go home but there was nowhere else to go. When he let himself into the house he stood still and listened. He would have found it hard to say what he was listening for, but recently the house had changed its character. It was no longer inanimate, passive, but a living, breathing presence which was sometimes hostile, sometimes approving.

The grandfather clock in the hall struck six. He went into the dining room and switched on the radio. He had to wait for the national news to end, then came the local news:

'In connection with the murder of Mr Kenneth Jobling, an insurance consultant, the police are anxious to talk to anyone who was in the neighbourhood of Commercial Road last night. The police emphasise that negative evidence is often of value and they wish to hear from people who were in the vicinity whether or not they saw or heard anything unusual. The number to ring is 222333 or call at any police station.

'Mr Jobling was attacked with a hammer or similar weapon and battered about the head. It seems that he was due in London on Friday night and that he set out to catch the 6.33 train for Paddington. How he came to be in Commercial Road later that evening is a mystery.'

He had not switched on any lights and it was almost dark; he stood thinking what he would do, then he went through to the hall, picked up the telephone and dialled the number of Jobling's flat. He heard the ringing tone five or six times before the receiver was lifted.

'774636.'

It was Jean's voice; if it had been Elizabeth's he would have spoken.

He replaced the receiver. The sound of the front door bell startled him and he took a moment to compose himself before answering it. It was his neighbour, Mrs Lambert. She peered past him into the darkness.

'I heard you come home but I didn't see any lights.'

He said nothing.

'Two men came about half past five, not long before you got back. I told them you were out and they said they would come again.'

'Two men?'

'I think they were policemen.' She looked at him directly for the first time.

He was still sufficiently in control to cope with Mrs Lambert. 'Oh, yes, I made a complaint this morning and I expect they came about that.'

He started to shut the door and she moved off. He went into the lounge, which had scarcely been used since Jean left, and stood by the window watching the road. He could not have said how long he remained there but he began to feel chilled and stiff. In the end he could stand the waiting no longer. He

61

went into the hall, put on his raincoat and went through to the garage. A few minutes later he was driving along the route he had walked the night before. He passed the pub in Bewdley Street, came out into Commercial Road, parked his car and walked across to the wall overlooking the canal. He stood with his arms resting on the granite coping looking down at the water. Away to his right he could see the lights of the green and after a little while he started to walk in that direction. He crossed the bridge over the canal and as he was entering the café he glanced up at Gladbrook House, where he thought he could see lights on the second floor. The café was empty except for the girl behind the counter. She smiled at him but said nothing.

'Coffee, please.' He added while she was working the machine, 'Not very busy.'

'Too early.'

'Don't you ever get any time off?'

'Why? Was you thinking to ask me out?'

He took his coffee to the same table by the window.

'Do you live out this way?' She seemed to be in a mood for conversation.

'No, a long way from here.'

'I suppose you've heard about our murder?'

'Yes.'

'I had the fuzz in here just now.'

'The fuzz?'

'Police. They were asking who was in here last night and they wanted to know if I saw anything.'

His throat was dry. 'Saw anything?'

'Well, I might have. The boss came at eleven to cash up then I left. I live in Canal Street, just off Commercial Road. I could have passed him.'

She came to stand by his table, looking through the steamy window. 'They reckon that he was knocked off between nine and ten somewhere else, then his body was brought to Commercial Road in a car and dumped over the wall.'

He was conscious of her proximity and of a slightly sour smell which emanated from her blue overall.

'This afternoon they towed a caravan into the park. You can see its lights from here, just inside the gates. The copper who came here said it was a sort of mobile nick for the chaps working on the murder.'

He was unnaturally excited and his words came with difficulty. 'Did you tell them I was here last night?'

'Well, I couldn't, could I? I've got no memory, people who come in here are just customers, all alike.'

She reached over and, with the rag she carried, wiped the condensation from the window. As she did so he slid his hand up inside her thigh, along the silky material of her tights. She looked down at him.

'Well, I never! You can't go by looks and that's a fact!'

He was horribly embarrassed. 'I'm sorry ... I don't know what came over me ... I really don't know....'

'No harm done. What's the matter with you? Drink your coffee.'

'No, I must go.' He fumbled for his change, his face burning. 'I'm very sorry, I've never done anything like that before.'

As he closed the door he saw that she was watching him and she looked amused.

He walked rapidly away from the café regardless of direction and continued to walk until his heart-beat returned to normal and the intolerable burning of his face and ears had subsided. What happened was so unexpected and inexplicable that he was frightened.

By the time he was calm he had walked a considerable distance along the road which would have taken him to the city centre. The only thing to do was to return to the green, collect his car and drive home.

He put the car away and went through the communicating door into the house. He did not switch on the lights but stood in the darkness of the hall. Tonight the mood of the house was receptive and consoling. He made a mug of cocoa and took it up to bed with him. As he took his watch off he was astonished to see that it was still only half past nine. He lay in bed staring at the ceiling, where the light from a street lamp, shining between the curtains, made a geometrical pattern. He knew that he would have difficulty in going to sleep, but he could not take his tablets because he had not had the prescription made up.

He could not forget those naked, contorted bodies in the

film and his imagination insisted on providing detail which had not been explicit on the screen. Then there was the girl in the café. After all, it was not such a terrible thing he had done. She had looked at him in surprise, but also with tolerance and understanding.

'No harm done, is there? Drink your coffee.'

Probably she would have allowed him to go much further.

For much of his life he had been struggling against ... against what? Perhaps against himself and there are no prizes for that.

Arthur Milton, M.A., 16 Barnfield Close. Occupation: Schoolmaster. Head of the History Department, The Mercers' School. ...

A solid citizen.

All he had to do was to let go. Perhaps he was unnecessarily afraid of the demons lurking on the fringe of his consciousness, threatening to take possession. Perhaps they were not demons after all and had as much right to him as this hypocritical schoolmaster who scuttled away from reality like a scared mouse.

Chapter Five

HE WOKE LATE, when it was already broad daylight, and for a moment it seemed that he had slipped back through the years to a time when Elizabeth was a little girl. He fancied that he heard her in the next room talking to her dolls with a carefully enunciated lisp.

This sort of thing had happened several times recently and he had had vivid dreams recalling disturbing incidents long forgotten.

He put on his dressing gown and went downstairs to make himself a cup of tea. The grandfather clock struck nine while he was waiting for the kettle to boil. He heard the clinking of milk bottles and a few moments later he saw the milkman through the glass of the back door. The man looked at him with no sign of acknowledgement. He had a soreness at the base of his skull and his neck was stiff, probably because he had been tumbling about most of the night.

There was a ring at the front door bell. He was going to ignore it, but whoever it was rattled the letter-box with impatience. He went to the door, considerably irritated.

'Yes?'

Two men, one a blond, young man.

'Police.' The smaller of the two, middle-aged and haggard, who looked as though he had slept in his clothes, held out his warrant card. 'Detective Sergeant Hammond, this is Detective Constable Symons. Can we come in?'

'It's not very convenient, as you can see I've just got up.'

Hammond brushed this aside. 'Don't worry about that, Mr Milton, we're not fussy.'

Milton did not want these men in his house. 'If you want to talk to me I would rather come down to the station.'

Hammond's mobile features creased in exaggerated surprise. 'You surely don't mean to obstruct the police, Mr Milton?

I'm a busy man; it's Sunday, I ought to be home taking the kids out for a walk, bathing the dog or papering the spare bedroom; instead of that I've come here to talk to you and you won't see me. Is that it?'

He knew that he was being treated like a fool but he did not want to prolong the scene on the doorstep.

'All right, come in. The room on the right.'

He followed the two detectives into the sitting-room, where the curtains were still drawn.

'Bit dark in here, isn't it? Do you mind?' Hammond swished back the curtains and let in the cold morning light.

Milton felt angry; he was being bullied, an experience he had not known since his schooldays.

'Please tell me what you want; why you are here.'

'I think you know why we're here, Mr Milton. Kenneth Jobling has been murdered.'

'What is that to do with me?'

Hammond sat down in an armchair without being invited and looked round at the furniture as though he was about to make a bid for it.

'Look at it like this, Mr Milton: a couple of weeks ago your wife and daughter left you and went to live with this bloke. Yesterday we found him lying in a ditch by the tow-path with his head bashed in.'

'You can't think that I—?'

'I don't think anything, Mr Milton; we've got brainy chaps back at the nick to do all that. I just ask questions.'

'All right, tell me what you want to know.'

'Have you heard from your wife since it happened?'

'No.'

'Nor from your daughter?'

'No.'

'Odd, don't you think?'

'No, I don't.'

'They might want to come back.'

'Can we get on with the questions?'

Hammond took a bent cigarette from his pocket, carefully straightened and lit it.

'You don't mind if Bob sits down, do you Mr Milton?'

Milton did not answer and the constable, who had been

standing by the door, sat on the settee.

'Surely you resented your wife leaving you for another man?'

'I was upset, naturally.'

'Very naturally. Were you sufficiently upset to try to get her back?'

'I tried to see her.'

'You went to Jobling's flat?'

'Yes.'

'But she wouldn't see you and you were so angry that you assaulted Jobling.'

'That's not true!' He was becoming excited and stumbled over his words. 'If my wife told you that—'

Hammond knocked ash from his cigarette in the direction of the gas fire.

'Don't get worked up, Mr Milton. Your wife didn't tell us, we got that from an independent witness, the porter at the flats.'

'But I did not assault Jobling. I tried to get in to speak to Jean and he tried to stop me. There was a scuffle ... If you'd been in my position....'

Hammond grinned. 'If I'd been in your position I'd have punched him on the nose, but I wouldn't have gone back a couple of weeks later to clobber him with a two-pound hammer.'

Milton was watching the sergeant as though mesmerised. 'They said in the paper and on the radio that Jobling was the victim of a mugging, that he had been assaulted and robbed.' His manner was almost pleading.

'Reporters! They use their imaginations, they don't wait for facts. Jobling wasn't mugged or robbed, Mr Milton, you can take that from me. He was murdered by somebody who had a grudge and we have to ask ourselves who that might be. As a wronged husband you're an odds-on chance.'

'But....'

'Where were you on Friday night, Mr Milton?'

'Friday? That was the evening I went to see my doctor.'

'Oh? Why was that?'

'I wasn't feeling well, I wanted a check-up.'

'Not surprising. Which doctor?'

67

'Dr Evans in Manor Park Road.'

'What time did you leave there?'

'About half past seven.'

'And then?'

'Then?'

Hammond shifted impatiently in his chair. 'Don't play games, Mr Milton. Where did you go after you left the doctor's?'

'I stood for a while watching the bonfire on the waste ground at the end of Manor Park Road then I came back here and spent the rest of the evening until I went to bed.'

'What time did you get back here?'

'About half past eight.'

'Were you walking or did you take your car?'

'I was walking.'

The constable who had not spoken and had scarcely moved, suddenly sneezed violently. Hammond looked at him with disapproval. There was silence which seemed to last a long time. Hammond crushed out the stub of his cigarette in his matchbox.

'You are quite sure that you did not see Jobling on Friday night?'

'Quite sure.'

Hammond brushed ash from his jacket and stretched his legs. 'Between you and me, Mr Milton, we don't think that he was killed in Commercial Road. We think he was killed in some workshop or garage, then his body was taken in a car to Commercial Road and dumped over the wall on to the tow-path.'

Milton said nothing.

'He had a dirty great oil stain right across the back of his raincoat just as though he'd been leaning back against an oily bench. Funny thing for a natty dresser like him to do, don't you think?'

'I suppose so, I don't know anything about him.'

'The soles of his shoes were oily too and they found bits of metal sticking to the oil—filings. The lab boys say some of the filings were iron and the others an aluminium alloy.'

Milton remained silent.

'What sort of car is yours?'

'A Marina.'

'What colour?'

'Dark blue.'

'And you keep it in the garage?'

'Of course.'

Hammond nodded, staring out of the window where starlings were hopefully quartering the grass. 'Do you use your garage to do odd jobs? Have you got a bench there? Tools? A vice, say?'

'Yes, I've got a bench with a vice. I like to do small household jobs.'

'Takes your mind off things, eh?'

'I like working with my hands.'

'Good! Let's have a look at this garage, shall we?' He stood up.

Milton led the way into the hall and through the communicating door into the garage. Hammond went to the bench, ran his hand along it and examined the floor.

'Had a clean-up recently?'

'Not recently, no.'

'I'd like to borrow your car, Mr Milton.'

'*Borrow* it?'

'Just to have a look and see if you've been carting any bodies about. If you haven't it should do you a bit of good, might even get you off the hook.'

'Can't you look at it here?'

Hammond grinned. 'We are only messenger boys, really. They use the brainy chaps to examine cars and things like that. If all goes well you'll have it back this evening.'

'All right.'

'Perhaps you'll let the constable have your keys.'

Milton fetched his car key. 'The garage door opens from the inside.'

'Leave it to him, Mr Milton, he's not as thick as he looks.'

Hammond continued to stand by the bench; he took down a hammer from the rack of tools.

'What sort of hammer is that, Mr Milton?'

'I think they call it a claw hammer or maybe a carpenter's hammer.'

'You don't seem to have a ball-and-peen hammer in your outfit.'

'I don't know what it is.'

Hammond shook his head. 'Neither did I until yesterday. It's a hammer used by metal workers with a flat face at one end and a ball at the other. According to the pathologist, Jobling probably had his temple smashed in with the ball-end of one of those.'

Milton said nothing. The constable had the garage door open and was getting into the car. Hammond led the way back into the house. He stood in the hall by the grandfather clock.

'You're a big chap, Mr Milton, taller than I am, and you look in fairish condition.'

'If you've finished asking me questions—'

'Jobling was only a little fellow, pot-bellied too. Beats me why your wife left you for him.'

'I don't think you have the right to behave in this insulting—'

'He wouldn't have stood much chance if you went for him with one of those ball-and-peen hammers, Mr Milton, would he?'

'But I've told you—'

'Of course you have, you mustn't let me upset you. What's this, then?' He had crossed the hall and pushed open the door of Milton's study.

'That's my room where I work.'

'Very nice too. I wish I had a place where I could get away from the kids. I've got two girls—nine and eleven and devils both of 'em.'

He was looking round the study and two photographs caught his attention. 'Oh, there they are, your wife and your daughter. I've met 'em both. Very nice. Anyway, I expect you'll soon have 'em back.'

'Mr Hammond, if you've finished with me....'

'Yes, okay. I'll be off. You'll have your car back this evening unless we find you've been carting bodies around or driving without a road-fund licence.'

Hammond laughed at his own joke. He let himself out and stood with the front door open.

70

'If you have second thoughts about anything, Mr Milton, come and see me.'

He had only a vague recollection of how he got through the rest of Sunday. He could not remember having a meal and he seemed to spend a good deal of his time wandering about the house. The police visit had profoundly disturbed him, and not only because he was suspected of having killed Jobling. They had taken possession of his house and humiliated him.

At seven o'clock in the evening a young constable returned his car.

'Well?'

'Well what, sir?'

'Are they satisfied?'

'I don't know anything about it, sir. I was just told to bring your car back.'

He tried to read, but his mind refused to interpret what he read and he found himself going over the same lines again and again. In the end he snapped the book shut and went up the stairs to bed.

'A-T-O-N-E-M-E-N-T.' He spelt out the word under his breath. He had no idea why he did so or precisely what it was for which he must atone. Often, lately, he seemed to be fighting a battle to maintain an orderly progression of thought, to hold himself together, and he sometimes found relief in speaking a word aloud or even spelling it out, letter by letter.

On Monday morning there was an assembly of the whole upper school. He stood with other staff at the entrance to the main hall, watching the girls and boys file past. It began with the fourths, then the fifths, but he was waiting anxiously for the sixth forms, for Elizabeth. When they came she was not among them. Perhaps she had stayed at home to comfort Jean. Perhaps Jean would not allow her to come because ... For the first time it occurred to him that Jean might keep Elizabeth from him because she believed that he had killed Jobling. The idea came to him as such a surprise that he remained standing for a moment after the others had followed the headmaster into the hall.

At break in the staff common-room he was aware of a constraint among the people near him. It was evident that they were trying to make conversation and finding it hard going. The climax came when, in one of those inexplicable silences which suddenly fall on a crowded room, a voice was clearly heard: 'Of course, the police think Milly killed the poor bastard....'

He would have done better to stay where he was, to pretend that he had not heard or not understood; instead he got up and stalked through the room, drawing everybody's attention. His heart-beat was alarming and the throbbing in his head seemed to cloud his vision, but he went on. Somebody opened the door for him and he went along the corridor through a milling mass of boys and girls to the history prep-room. Pray God it was empty. There were three members of staff attached to his department and any one of them might be there. He pushed open the door and found only the boy Wilson, standing by the bookshelves, looking at the titles. It was too much.

'Get out!' His voice was distorted with anger and something near to tears.

The boy looked at him strangely. 'Mr Collins told me to wait for him here, sir. I'm due for a special lesson.'

'Get out! Get out! Do you hear me? Get out!'

He was almost screaming and the boy fled. Milton looked after him and saw Bates, the headmaster, standing in the corridor. For once Bates was at a loss; Milton slammed the door in his face.

At lunchtime he did not go to the dining-hall but remained in the prep-room, and it was there that Bates ran him to earth. Bates was agitated but striving to appear calm.

'Ah, there you are, Arthur, I've been looking all over. I wonder if you would come up to my room for a word?'

'We can talk just as well here.'

'As you wish.'

Bates opened the door and shut it again, as though by doing so he ensured their privacy. Then he perched himself on a stool, because Milton had the only chair.

'I know that things are bad with you at the moment, Arthur, and I'm sorry, but I also know that it will all come right in the end.'

'Thank you.'

72

'Don't you think it would be a good idea to take some time off? Have a break of a week or two ... You would continue to draw your full salary.'

'You must have been speaking to Chudleigh.' Sir George Chudleigh was chairman of the governors.

Bates looked embarrassed. 'Well, yes, I had a word with Sir George; he was very understanding.'

'What about County Hall?'

Bates knew that he was being attacked but there was nothing he could do. 'I don't understand.'

'I'm asking you what the director said when you spoke to him.'

'Oh, he was equally helpful.'

'He would be. We can't have a murderer teaching our children.'

'My dear Arthur, I do wish you would believe that I have acted as much in your interest as for the good of the school.'

'Do I leave now or take my afternoon classes?'

'Well, Arthur, there's no point in spinning it out. Don't get too depressed about all this though. You'll be back with us again in a week or two as though nothing had happened.'

Milton stood up so that he was looking down on Bates. 'Either you are a fool or you think I am.'

In a way it was a relief.

He spent the afternoon going through the cupboards in the department and removing everything which belonged to him. Several times in the course of twenty years teaching he had seen colleagues on the point of retirement doing the same thing and had wondered how they felt. The finality of this prosaic operation intrigued him. Three or four times he went out to his car with books, charts and piles of manuscript notes. It was odd the things one accumulated. A former head of maths had been seen to go out with a teddy bear.

On one of his trips he met Bates. Bates was on the point of making some protest—'This really isn't necessary, old man!' —but he changed his mind, shrugged and walked on.

As he drove home that evening Milton realised that what had happened was necessary, perhaps inevitable.

Sometimes he felt that everything was on the point of becoming clear, of crystallising out. He had read how mathematicians and scientists may live with a number of seemingly unconnected ideas for weeks or months or even years; then, suddenly, without conscious effort, a pattern emerges which relates them in a lucid and compellingly logical way. Koestler calls these unconscious processes of the mind, underground games.

The boy Wilson, his sister in the photograph, Jean's unspoken taunts, his ambivalent relationship with Elizabeth, his visit to the flat in Gordon Street and, above all, his growing sense of guilt and of the need to atone. Twenty years of his life. There must be a key to the pattern and one day, soon. . . .

He realised that he was very hungry; he had had no lunch and he had eaten little the day before. Usually he bought what he wanted in a shopping precinct near the house on his way home from school, but today he had not done so. It was almost five, but the shops did not close until half past. He put on his coat and, taking his shopping bag, let himself out by the front door. The butcher did not open on Mondays, but there was a delicatessen which was also an off-licence, and the fat woman who ran it had become almost a friend. From the first day after Jean left and he had been forced to do his own shopping she had taken him under her wing. She was the one person who could refer to his situation without offending him.

Her first remark, when he did not even know her, had been: 'Well, you're on your own now and a man on his own has to take care of himself. Never mind about the cleaning and the dusting, but make sure you get one decent meal inside you every day.'

Another time it was: 'You don't want too much frying pan. The butcher next door has some nice chuck steak. Get half a pound of that and cut it up into small cubes. . . .'

But tonight even the fat woman was reserved, cautious. A man deserted by his wife is one thing, a murderer is quite another.

'Good evening, Mrs Latham.'

'Good evening.'

'I thought I might have a few sausages.'

'Pork or beef?' Tight lipped.

74

'Oh, pork, I think.'

She picked up a half-pound pack and slipped it into a bag.

He felt adventurous. 'What's this Italian wine like?'

'All right as far as I know.'

'I'll take a bottle.'

'That's one pound fifty two.'

He felt snubbed.

As he turned the corner into his own road he saw the police car parked by his house, and as he drew nearer he could see two men in it. He almost decided to turn tail and run, but where could he go? He recognised Hammond and the fair young constable who had been with him the previous day.

'You know Constable Symons. We'd better go inside.'

If Milton had thought of protesting he did not do so. Hammond looked grim and tired. In the lounge he did not waste time on formalities; he even switched on the light without a by-your-leave.

'Last night you gave me an account of your movements on Friday evening. You said that you went to your doctor and that you returned here at half past eight, is that right?'

'That is what I told you.' Milton put his sausages and his bottle of wine on a coffee table.

'But it wasn't the truth, was it?' Hammond lit a cigarette. 'It's a dangerous game to tell lies in a murder case, Mr Milton. At best it's a waste of police time, at worst it could land you into very serious trouble.'

Hammond was lounging in one of the armchairs. The constable was standing by the door, almost as though they were afraid he might make a bolt for it.

Milton could not bring himself to sit down.

'I ...'

'Before you say anything—and you don't have to—think carefully and make up your mind that anything you do decide to tell me is the truth.'

'Is that an official warning?'

'You know damn well it isn't. It's a friendly tip, but you'd be a fool not to take notice.' He lit a cigarette.

'I didn't want to get involved, I had nothing to hide.'

75

'You are involved and it looks very much as though you had something to hide.'

'When I left the doctor I was upset and I went for a walk.'

'Where?'

'I walked without taking any notice of where I was going. I went into a public house.'

'The Bewdley Arms, just off Commercial Road.'

'Yes, I didn't know when I went in but I saw Bewdley Street on the corner of a house when I came out.'

'You were seen and recognised in the pub but you stayed only a few minutes. That was between half past eight and nine. What did you do then?'

'I walked up Commercial Road to the green and I went in the little café there.'

'What time was that?'

'It must have been about nine o'clock.'

'Did you see anybody in Commercial Road?'

'No, it was deserted—wait a minute—there was a police car, it passed me and I thought the driver slowed down.'

'Nothing else?'

'No.'

'At what time did you leave the café?'

'At eleven o'clock when they closed.'

'But the girl in the café says that she didn't see you there on Friday evening.'

A curious look of satisfaction passed over Milton's face and puzzled the sergeant.

'I don't suppose she noticed me; she was busy.'

'You sat there for two hours and she didn't notice you?'

'Well, she can't have done, can she?'

Hammond flicked ash on the carpet.

'Think again, Mr Milton, what were you doing between nine and eleven on Friday evening?'

Milton's face set in hard, obstinate lines. Nothing would make him speak of the time he had spent in a shop doorway waiting for his daughter, or of seeing her with the boy.

'I've told you.'

Hammond sighed and stood up. 'Very well, I'll accept that for the moment but remember that it was during those two hours that Jobling was killed. I'm going now but I shall be back.'

This time the sergeant did not bother with even the sketchiest courtesy. The front door slammed behind them.

Milton felt chilled inside and out. The house seemed foreign and hostile; even in his study he felt like a stranger. His privacy had been invaded and finally destroyed.

They were taking everything away from him, his wife, his daughter, his job and now his home. Yet even as he indulged in self-pity he knew that he was to blame, that he had brought all this on himself. He was a victim, but only of his own actions. He was reminded of Poe's story, 'Imp of the Perverse' but stifled the recollection at once in an access of something near panic.

'I am P-O-S-S-E-S-S-E-D.'

He knew that it was nonsense, but how else to explain or even describe the feeling that he was being driven along in a course of action which he had not chosen and could not control?

'What, exactly, are you afraid of?'

'Of guilt.'

'Of what are you guilty?'

'I don't know.'

The questions needed to probe more deeply, to begin further back. What he needed was a priest, a priest with a fat belly, complacent in worldliness yet retaining compassion. But he was not religious, certainly not Christian. The secular equivalent of a priest is a psychiatrist, but he distrusted psychiatrists, their smooth, slick pseudo-science and their jargon with its medieval flavour. Lapping up the secrets of the soul as a greedy cat laps up milk.

'I charge thee come out of him!'

That was better, but you have to have faith.

'The psycho-analyst induces his patient to relive his conflicts, to make the unconscious conscious, *to bring to light unsatisfied tensions and to allow their expression without guilt. . . .'*

He remembered that from a paperback.

Feeling unusually lucid, he went upstairs and started to pack a suitcase. A spare jacket and trousers, underclothes, pyjamas, slippers, razor ... Downstairs again he wrote a note for the milkman and enclosed a small sum to cover what he owed. This done he put on his raincoat and let himself out by the front door.

It had scarcely stopped raining all day, and the roads were dark and shining under the street lamps. He caught a bus to the city centre and another to Palmerston Green. He got out at the bank and, keeping close to the buildings, walked briskly round the corner to the café. He avoided looking across to the lights of the police caravan just inside the park railings. As usual the window of the café was steamed over and he opened the door in clumsy haste for fear that she would not be there, but she was, elbows on the counter.

Two tables were occupied: at one a man and a woman were finishing off a cooked meal of some sort; at the other, a fat woman with red hair and wearing a plum-coloured raincoat, had a Chelsea bun and a pot of tea.

The girl's lips flickered into a half smile. 'Back again?'

He felt as though he had come home, but he stood at the counter sheepish and inarticulate.

'Do you want something to eat or just coffee?'

'I'm hungry, I think.'

She laughed as though he had said something funny and he felt warm inside.

'The liver's not bad, you can have it with sausages or with egg and bacon.'

'Liver and bacon would be nice.'

'Chips?'

'A few.'

'One liver-and-bacon-small-chips, Florrie,' she called through the hatch.

So the cook was a woman, not a man as he had thought. He was pleased to be wrong.

Without asking him she filled a cup of coffee and passed it over. 'To be going on with.'

He took his coffee to the usual table by the window. She had good features and a clear, smooth skin. He had noticed her eyes; they were very dark brown and he would have liked them even better if she had not worn eye-shadow. Her hair was brown, soft looking, and as she moved her head it seemed to linger with a sensuous inertia. He could not understand why he had thought her plain.

The couple had finished their meal. 'Bill, please, Miss.'

She went over to them with her pad and pencil. 'One pound twenty-four.'

'One pound twenty-four? How d'you make that out?' The woman was prepared to be aggressive. The girl slipped the bill on the table between them.

'It's all there, see for yourself.'

While they were studying the bill she looked across at him and winked.

'I'll have another one of they buns, Miss. Bit dry though, aren't they? What about a bit of butter?'

'Threepence a pat.'

'Threepence? You know what you can do with that, young woman.' She turned to Milton. 'Did you 'ear that? Threepence for a piddling bit of butter! That's nigh on eightpence in the old money!'

The girl got a bun from the glass shelves on the counter, put it on a plate and slapped the plate on the table. The couple paid and went. The cook rapped on the hatch and she went to fetch his meal.

'There you are, all nice and hot.'

She stood by his table as he began to eat and once more he caught the slightly sour smell from her overall.

'Going away?'

He looked up, startled by her question.

'Your bag.'

'Oh, that. I was thinking of coming out this way to stay for a while. I don't suppose you know of anybody with a room to let?'

'Not that would suit you.'

'Why wouldn't it suit me?'

'Well, you'd want something a bit posh—hotel or something.'

'No, I want somewhere very simple and plain where I can be quiet.'

She frowned. 'I don't know about that.'

'About what?'

'Well, my mother lets rooms, mostly to lorry drivers. Just bed and breakfast. But things are slack just now.'

He was suddenly very excited. 'But that would suit me very well.' He hesitated. 'Would your mother let me stay in the room during the day?'

She laughed. 'You could die there as long as you paid.'

'Well, if you'll tell me where you live, I'll get along there and book my room.' He was getting up from his seat, leaving the meal he had scarcely begun.

She laughed again. 'Finish your liver, you don't have to worry. Last night we had three rooms empty and Mondays is worse. We haven't been full since the spring.'

'Well, that's splendid, I'm very grateful.'

She looked down at him and shook her head. 'I hope you will be when you see it.' But he felt that there was now a very special relationship between them, a particular intimacy. He saw the red-haired woman watching them with her beady little eyes and he was glad.

He finished his meal and had another cup of coffee, then he asked her where she lived.

'Canal Street, number twenty-one. If you go out of here and down Commercial Road, the first turning off is Bewdley Street and the next is our street. Our house is half-way up on the left. You can't miss it because there's a sign saying we cater for transport.' She hesitated. 'If you don't like it when you see it, don't take it. You can tell mother I sent you.'

She came with him to the door and called after him. 'Down Commercial Road, second on the left. See you later!'

He raised his hand and felt almost gay.

He passed the bottom of Bewdley Street and continued along past more warehouses to the next turning. A street lamp lit the sign: Canal Street. It was not much different from Bewdley Street, a little wider but the same brick-built houses with starved front gardens from which the railings had been removed during the war. Number twenty-one was double-fronted and the fan-light over the door was lit up and lettered: 'Transport Drivers Catered For'.

He rang the bell in the glass-panelled door, and after a short while he saw the vague outline of a figure on the other side of the hammered glass. The door opened and he was confronted by a plump woman in a black skirt and lacy

80

see-through blouse. She was heavily made up and her scent came at him in waves.

'What can I do for you?'

'I am looking for a room.'

She seemed surprised. 'One night?'

'For a week at least, if that's all right.' He added, after a moment, 'Your daughter recommended me to come here.'

'Julie? Well, I never!' She eyed him a little more. 'You know I only do room and breakfast—no lunch or evening meal?'

'Yes, that would suit me very well.'

'You'd better come in.'

The little hall was covered with shiny linoleum in a pattern of wood blocks. She opened a door on the right and switched on a light.

'This is the dining-room where we serve breakfast.'

There were five or six tables with green, plastic tops, each provided with salt and pepper pots and a sauce bottle.

'I'm not sure that this is your sort of place.'

'I think it will do very well.' He had difficulty in knowing where to look, for her breasts were clearly visible through her blouse.

She was still dubious. 'You'd better see your room.'

He followed up a flight of steep stairs covered with a floral linoleum. She hesitated on the landing, then pushed open one of several doors and switched on the light.

A bed covered with a brown quilt, green lino on the floor, a mat by the bed, a match-wood wardrobe with a mirror, a table with two drawers and a wicker chair with a grubby chintz cushion.

'Yes, thank you, that's fine.'

'There's a gas fire on the meter. Tenpenny pieces.'

'Very convenient.'

She looked at him to see if he was being sarcastic. 'The toilet and bathroom are labelled. If you want a bath it's fifteen pence—in advance.'

'Good, I'll take it.'

'Don't you want to know how much? It's two pounds twenty for a night or twelve pounds fifty for the week *and* I want a deposit.'

81

He took out his wallet and offered her a ten-pound note.

'Thanks, I'll give you a receipt.'

'There's no need.'

'Well, if you're satisfied. . . .'

'Quite satisfied, thank you.'

'I'll be getting along then. As a matter of fact there's a programme on the telly.'

'I'm sorry.'

'Don't mention it.' She paused with her hand on the door knob. 'I don't mind you coming down to my sitting room if you want to any time, provided I haven't got company.'

'That's very kind of you, Mrs. . . .'

'Grace, Nellie Grace. I'm a widow.'

'My name is Stuart—Charles Stuart.' It was the first name that came into his head.

She went at last and he was left alone in his little room. He lit the gas fire and put his few belongings in the wardrobe, then he sat in the wicker chair. It was nine o'clock. His thoughts seemed to be racing, but he wasn't thinking anything. It must have been the sudden change in his circumstances. Incredible that it could have been achieved in so short a time.

He must have fallen asleep in the wicker chair, for he was awakened by a tap on the door. For a moment he could not think where he was. It was Julie, and for the first time he saw her without her overall. She looked quite different in jeans and a woolly sweater, at the same time more appealing and more remote.

'It's all right, then?'

She seemed amused, as though she were indulging a child in a game. She went over to the bed and pulled back the bedclothes.

'I thought as much, she hasn't changed the bed.'

She went out again, leaving the bed tumbled, but she was soon back with a pile of linen. Bedding was scattered over the floor and in a surprisingly short time the bed was remade.

'There now, at least you won't be sleeping in somebody else's dirt.'

'Thank you.'

'Like some cocoa?'

He had gone to bed and was dozing off when he heard sounds from the next room. A door opened, the floor creaked under heavy footsteps and a man coughed, a real smoker's cough. Milton heard him pouring water from the carafe on his dressing table; the partitions were so thin he might have been in the same room. The bed springs creaked as he sat on the bed to take off his shoes. Milton could follow the progress of his undressing, even hear the suppressed grunt as he stooped to pick something off the floor. Finally he heard him get into bed, shift his position two or three times, then settle down.

There was silence for several minutes, then the door opened again.

'I'd given you up.'

As far as Milton knew there were only two women in the house and he waited in suspense to hear the newcomer's voice.

'Aren't you coming to bed? What are you lighting the fire for?'

'I like a bit of comfort, Charlie.'

Milton had been holding his breath, now he released it in a great spasm of relief.

'What you got that thing on for?'

'For you to take off ... Be careful, you great ape! You're like a greedy kid unwrapping a sweet.'

'Some sweet! More like a fat little pig.'

'Bastard!'

'Don't worry, you won't hear me complaining.'

Milton had no option but to listen. As they approached the climax of their love-making his body became rigid and he lay in a state of almost unbearable tension, bathed in sweat.

When it was over he felt bitterly ashamed and promised himself that he would change his room or leave.

Chapter Six

HE SLEPT WELL in the end, and when he woke it was beginning to get light. Charlie was moving about in the next room and indulging in fits of coughing. There was a smell of frying bacon. He got out of bed and went to the bathroom, but the door was locked so he returned to his room and sat on the bed waiting. He had to wait about ten minutes.

When he had washed and dressed he went downstairs to the dining room, where two men in thick polo-necked sweaters were having breakfast. They looked at him without interest. A large, circular oil-stove gave out a stuffy warmth.

He felt that he was being carried along, unresisting, to some climax, and the sensation was not altogether unpleasant. Things had been taken out of his hands, but at the same time his senses seemed to have become dulled; sights and sounds reached him through some indefinable barrier as though he were under the effects of a mild anaesthetic.

Julie's mother brought him his breakfast.

'Sleep well?'

'Yes, thank you.'

'These are two of my regulars, Mr Stuart. They've been coming here for years whenever they're this way.'

She lingered near his table, making him feel uncomfortable, and he thought that she was watching him with the same tolerant amusement he had seen in the eyes of her daughter.

She seemed to answer his thought:

'Her ladyship doesn't get up until the last minute. She has to be at work by ten and at five to you'd think a typhoon had gone through the place'

He felt disappointed but said nothing.

'Is your coffee all right?'

'Yes, thank you.'

He wondered which of the two men was Charlie.

After breakfast he spent some time in his room. It was cold and he was glad to sit over the gas fire. He had never lived in a street like this before, where the houses were on top of one another and people lived like rabbits in hutches. Even so there was little sign of life in the fronts of the houses opposite. Now and then a child set out for school from one or other of the houses, slamming the front door; a milk-float worked its way down the street, leaving one or two bottles on each doorstep. The postman followed.

He could not quite see the corner shop, but he could hear the 'ping' of its door bell.

The rain had stopped and there was fitful sunshine with drifting, fleecy white clouds.

At a quarter to ten he turned out the fire, made himself presentable and put on his raincoat. As he crossed the landing one of the doors opened and Julie came out, wearing a wrap, her eyes puffed with sleep. She brushed past him without a word and shut herself in the bathroom.

He walked to the end of the street and turned up Commercial Road in the direction of the green, but at the next junction he turned off again into Bewdley Street. He reached the pub, the Bewdley Arms, its doors closed and shuttered. He had not realised that almost all the houses on the pub side were empty and derelict, their windows boarded up or the frames gaping. The houses on the other side were still lived in.

He continued walking. Bewdley Street led into a more prosperous looking street of semi-detached houses with neat front gardens, and at the end of this the road forked. He took the right-hand fork and came to playing fields fringed with trees and surrounding a school. The school was a heterogeneous collection of buildings in stone, brick and concrete which had mushroomed over the years. At the entrance a weather-worn sign board read: 'Atherton Road Grammar School. Headmaster: G. A. Rowse, M.A.'. The word grammar had been ineffectually painted out.

From where he stood Milton could see into two or three of the classrooms, and on the top floor of one block boys and girls were working with scientific apparatus near one of the windows. He raised his hand to his face, half convinced that

85

a girl's hair had lightly brushed his cheek. He had a compelling desire to see the inside of the school. With no fixed idea as to what he would say if challenged he walked up the paved way to the swing doors, pushed open one of them and entered the foyer.

He had forgotten the smell. Schools have a generic smell but even so, each is subtly different from every other. This one came back to him with disturbing clarity as the first one in which he had recognised the smell of Girl.

There was a glass-fronted office to his right, where two women were working. That was new. While he was hesitating over whether to cross the foyer and walk boldly down the main corridor, a glass panel slid back and a voice called to him:

'Can I help you?'

He almost turned tail and fled, but that seemed to require more courage than brazening it out. He walked across to the office.

'I once taught here for a short time, twenty years ago, and I was curious to see the place again.' He added, after a moment, 'I was a student teacher then, only here for one term.'

The girl—she was no more than twenty-five—tried to be polite, 'That was before my time.'

'Yes, but the headmaster, Mr Rowse, was here then—he arrived the September before. . . .'

A door opened and a tall, heavily built man with a bald head came into the office. Milton met his gaze momentarily then turned away and went out through the swing doors. Rowse would not have remembered him from twenty years ago, but Milton had attended inter-schools meetings quite recently at which Rowse had been present.

He had made a fool of himself. If Rowse had recognised him he would be sure to ring up Bates at Mercers'.

'Milton? Oh, dear! The poor chap is off school because of his trouble . . . His wife left him and the man she went off with has been found murdered . . . Yes, that's right, by the canal . . . I don't know if they suspect him but he's certainly been questioned . . . But why on earth was he hanging around your place? . . . Told her what? . . . Student teacher—but was he ever a student teacher at Atherton Road? . . . I didn't know that. To be perfectly frank, I think this business has affected

86

his mind . . . No, I'm sure you don't, all the same, one doesn't want to take any chances . . . I quite agree. . . .'

Rowse would be disturbed. Even if he hadn't recognized him he would be concerned. Headmasters have no liking for strange men in raincoats hanging round their schools. He might even report the incident to the police.

He walked past the school and turned off the road along a footpath which skirted the playing fields, then entered a copse of elder and willow, bordering a tiny stream. The path was neglected—choked with decaying leaves, muddy and, in parts, flooded—but he plodded on, covering his shoes and trouser legs with mud.

'Did you want to speak to me, Christine?'

She used to stay behind after the others had gone. There would be some question about a comment he had written on her essay or a remark he had made in class. She would hang on his words with flattering attention. She was seventeen and he was twenty-two.

'You make everything so clear. I'm getting keen on history and I used to find it a bore. I only took it up to make a third A-level.'

She would go out with her books under her arm, demure, respectful.

He had had very little to do with girls at that time: an only child, a boys' school, and at university he was too busy to think about them, except sometimes at night.

But there was something wrong with his memory of Christine. Try as he would he could not resolve her features; the face he saw in his mind's eye was a disturbing hybrid which had something of Elizabeth and something of the girl in the café.

He shivered involuntarily and increased his pace.

The path petered out in a building site and he had to make his way through a network of newly-made roads with houses in all stages of construction. When he walked that way with Christine twenty years before there had been nothing but fields, and they had watched the cows tearing off great mouthfuls of grass with a satisfying ripping sound. It was after school and Christine was wearing her school uniform, including the regulation beret perched at a saucy angle on her fair curls. He could recall everything about her—except her face.

'We ought not to be doing this.'

'Why not?'

'Because you are a pupil and I'm a teacher.'

'But we're just out for a walk, it's not as though we were doing anything wrong.'

'All the same, I'd be in trouble if we were seen.'

'I'm not a child, I'm seventeen—over the age of consent.'

'Don't talk like that, Christine!'

'No, sir! Sorry, sir!'

They both laughed as though at the funniest joke imaginable.

He reached the main road, found a bus-stop and waited fifteen minutes for a bus to take him to the city centre. It was odd, being out and about when he should have been at school. At this very moment, eleven-fifteen, he should have been teaching a fifth form history set: Disraeli and the overthrow of Peel. It seemed incredible that only twenty-four hours before he had been following his routine with scarcely a thought of any possible alternative.

He was going to lunch in town, but when he got off at the city centre it was still only a quarter to twelve so he sauntered along the pavements looking in the shop windows. Once he thought that a policeman looked at him with more than passing interest, but he deliberately stared the man out before walking on. He had left his house and his job, he had changed his name, but he was not hiding.

'He's missing all right, sarge, he's done a bunk.'

Hammond and Symons were drinking foul coffee in one of the cubicles of the police caravan parked in the green.

'I went to see this Mrs....' He glanced at his notebook. 'Mrs Lambert, his next door neighbour. She says that not long after we left him last evening, he went out carrying a suitcase and she hasn't seen him since. This morning the milkman told her that he'd left a note, cancelling his milk. She thought it was odd and that she'd better tell us about it.'

'Nosey old bitch!'

'You could say that, sarge, or you could say that she was a responsible citizen, doing her duty.'

Hammond grinned. 'God help us! If you go on talking that way you'll end up by believing it.' He lit a second cigarette from the butt of the first. 'Anyway, have you tried the school?'

'First thing I did, I spoke on the phone to Bates, the headmaster, and asked if it was possible to have a word with Milton. He said that Milton had been granted leave of absence for an indefinite period.'

'Mr Goddard isn't going to like this.'

'Do the brass think he did it, sarge?'

'I don't know what they think, they don't confide in me.'

The telephone rang in the adjoining office and Hammond went to answer it. When he came back he looked relieved.

'That was the nick. One of the beat bobbies, on duty in the centre, happened to know that we were interested in Milton, and he's just come through on his personal radio to say that he's seen him. Apparently Milton teaches his kid, so he recognised him. A resourceful bloke. He's keeping an eye on Milton until further notice. At the time he called Milton was going into Bratt's, the stationers, opposite the town hall.'

'What do we do now, sarge?'

'What you do is take over from that bobby. Keep on to Milton without being too obvious about it and phone in when you can.'

'What about relief, sarge?'

Hammond looked at him with distaste. 'Relief from what?'

Across the square from the town hall there was a big stationers, a Mecca for people like Milton who derived the keenest pleasure from shelves filled with exercise books and box files, from trays of pens, pencils and spring-clips, from pots of glue and bottles of ink.

He felt sure that the ensuing days were going to be the most significant of his life and he had made up his mind to keep a record in which he would set down his actions and his thoughts. He had come away from home with the bare necessities of clothing and toilet articles, so he was going to buy himself a nice new exercise book and a ball-point pen.

He wanted a thick exercise book in stiff covers with a marbled pattern on the outside and a black spine. He might as well have asked for a silver ink-stand and sand box.

'These are the thickest exercise books we stock.'

Anaemic things in limp covers of some plastic material, cheap and shiny. But he had to be content. He also bought himself a needlessly expensive ball-point which was probably less efficient than those sold three-on-a-card for twenty pence.

He had lunch at a Chinese restaurant, and when he came out the first edition of the evening paper was on the streets.

TOW-PATH MURDER : ARREST SOON

He bought a paper and turned to the item which was at the bottom of the front page:

> In a statement this morning Detective Chief Superintendent Goddard said that he was delighted with the public response to his appeal. A great deal of very useful information had come in and every report had been followed up.
>
> Asked if he was satisfied with the progress of the case, the superintendent said that he was confident an arrest would be made. He could not say how soon because investigations were still in hand but he had no doubt of a successful outcome.

Milton did not know what to think, but he was disturbed. Perhaps after all he was wrong to parade himself in the streets. He would be more circumspect in future.

At two-fifteen he presented himself at the offices of the *City Chronicle*. He had to join a queue of people who were handing in small advertisements and when his turn came the girl said, 'Where's your copy?'

He explained that he was not handing in an advertisement but wanted to consult their files.

'You haven't been here before?'

'No.'

'Then you'd better fill out a form.'

He took the form to a table near the door.

'Issues you wish to consult ... Year ... Month ... Day ... Purpose.... Full Name and Address ...'

He entered August 1956 and left the day blank. He gave

his reason as 'research', his name as Charles Stuart and he invented an address.

He had to queue again to hand in the form and then wait while it was passed to higher authority. At last he was called.

'This way.'

He was admitted behind the counter, taken through a very large room where a great many people sat at desks, then upstairs, through a green baize door and into a dimly lit room where the walls were lined with glass-fronted bookcases. There were several chairs and tables; a young man in shirt sleeves was working at one, a plump girl, showing a lot of leg, at another.

His guide glanced along the shelves, dragged a pair of steps into position and reached down a bulky volume which she slammed on one of the tables.

'There you are. July to December 1956. You mustn't make marks or tear anything out.'

He turned the pages in batches until he reached the month of August then he started to work through page by page.

'British Nationals Leave Egypt' ... 'Nkrumah Demands Independence' ... But he found what he was looking for, an item on the front page of the issue dated Monday 20th.

GIRL FOUND DEAD
Murder Hunt

Mr and Mrs James Wilson of 16 Bewdley Street, returned from their holiday on Sunday evening to find their daughter, Christine, dead. The Wilsons had spent a week in Weston-super-Mare leaving seventeen-year-old Christine at home. They became concerned when they found their front door unlocked and their house apparently empty. In the kitchen a meal was set out for two people and appeared to have been there since the previous day.

Mr Wilson went upstairs and found his daughter's body on the bed in her parents' bedroom; she had been strangled. A murder investigation is being conducted by Detective Chief Inspector John Welsh of the City C.I.D.

Christine was a sixth-form pupil at Atherton Road Grammar School where she was studying French, English and History for her Advanced Level G.C.E. examinations. Mr

G. A. Rowse, the headmaster, described her as an excellent pupil who would almost certainly have gone to university next year.

Mrs Wilson, the girl's mother, has been detained in hospital, suffering from shock but Mr Wilson told our reporter that Christine was a quiet girl who rarely went out with boys. She was so reliable that when she said that she did not want to go on holiday with them they had no hesitation in leaving her in the house alone. Mr Wilson is of the opinion that his daughter was assaulted by a casual caller, a door-to-door salesman or a tramp.

Milton stared at the few lines of print as though mesmerised by them. He felt the blood draining from his head and realised that he was about to faint. He gripped the table and made a great effort to recover himself. Perhaps he let out an involuntary sound, for a moment later the plump girl was bending over him, wide eyed and solicitous.

'Are you all right? Would you like a glass of water?'

He was aware of the young man watching him with cool detachment and he felt embarrassed. He made reassuring noises, stood up a little unsteadily, and left. In the confusion he forgot the paper bag containing his exercise book and the girl caught him up on the stairs.

'You forgot this.'

He felt confused and depressed. He had intended to spend a good deal more time in the newspaper office, following the press reports of the investigation, but he knew that he would not have the courage to go back. He had an acute sense of immediate and personal loss, and as he made his way among the women shoppers he was muttering to himself, 'Elizabeth is not dead, she is at school, quite safe ... quite safe.'

Walking steadied his nerves.

He was passing Marks and Spencer's when he saw Jean coming out of the store carrying a shopping bag. He stopped abruptly and turned to look in a window but she had seen him.

'Arthur!'

She looked him up and down, noticed the mud on his

shoes and trousers and the fact that the collar of his raincoat was turned inwards.

'I thought ...' she began but broke off. 'The police told me that....'

'That I had run away?'

'That you had left the house.'

She was wearing a smart dove-grey coat with a fur collar which he had not seen before, but she was very pale and her eyes were swollen as though by recent weeping. He was conscious of her eyes, which betrayed the confusion of her emotions, bewilderment mixed with something that was akin to fear.

'If you are not at the house, where are you living?'

'So that you can tell your friends, the police?' It was childish and absurd but for a reason that he did not understand he wanted to hurt her.

They stood facing each other, tense and unable or not daring to put their thoughts into words.

After a while she said, foolishly, 'You're not at school.'

'I've been suspended.'

She shook her head slowly as though to deny her thoughts.

'Is Elizabeth all right?' He was still troubled by the strange confusion of ideas which had started in the newspaper office and he had to ask.

'She insisted on going back to school this morning.'

'Does she think that her father is a murderer?' He could not resist putting the question in its most dramatic form.

'I don't know what she thinks, she doesn't talk to me any more. She's desperately upset and I begged her to stay at home, but she would go.'

They were partly blocking the pavement, so that people had to edge round them. He felt that he must say something to ease the tension or end the confrontation, but he found it extraordinarily difficult to make the simple declaration: 'I did not kill him, Jean.'

It sounded lame and he saw that he had made little impression on her. He tried again. 'What is happening to me ... What I am doing has very little to do with you or with your leaving me. It all started a long time ago. ...'

She looked puzzled. 'I don't know what you're talking about.'

93

'I can't explain.'

'Are you trying to say that there is someone else?'

At first he did not grasp her meaning and when he did he found the question incredible.

'Of course not!'

'What, then?'

It was useless.

'Arthur, why don't you go to the police and—'

'Give myself up?'

She was irritated. 'I was going to say, get things straightened out. I mean, walking out as you did was bound to. . . .'

'Why don't you call them over?'

Two uniformed policemen were strolling down the opposite pavement. She followed his gaze and he saw from the change in her expression that the shot had gone home.

'But Arthur. . . .'

In the end he put a stop to it by simply walking on, leaving her standing.

'I shall never want her back.'

He knew now that it was true.

Chief Inspector John Welsh.

He remembered the name from the newspaper account of Christine's death. It gave him the germ of an idea, but he had had enough for the moment. Without any clear idea of how he would spend the rest of the day he made for the green. The weather had turned clear and cold, with a biting wind out of the north which had stripped the trees in the park of their few remaining leaves. There seemed to be activity round the police caravan but he kept his eyes averted.

He pushed open the door of the café with a tremulous anticipation which he had not known for twenty years, but there was a youth standing by the counter chatting with Julie. He wore a black leather jacket with a swastika and some initials on the back. Milton felt absurdly let down.

But she smiled at him.

'Hullo, where've you been?'

'Why?'

'You look as though you've just come from a rough house.'

'I've been walking.'

'Better you than me.'

The youth picked up some change from the counter. 'Okay. I'll be off. See ya.'

'Who's that?'

'Just a fella.'

'Boy friend?'

'You must be joking.'

He felt better.

'What will you have?'

'Coffee, please.'

'Anything to eat?'

'I'll have something later.'

'I shan't be here, it's my evening off. I finish at five.'

'Oh.'

She handed him his coffee and he stood by the counter to drink it.

'Going somewhere?'

'Nowhere special, why?'

He was trembling. 'I wondered if you would like to come out for a meal?'

She looked at him with a half-smile. 'You serious?'

'Of course. I hope you don't mind me asking you.'

'Why should I?'

'I'm so much older.'

'What difference does that make?'

He looked at the clock: it was ten minutes to five.

A big man came in. He wore a shapeless overcoat, open down the front; his trousers were held up by a broad leather belt with a brass buckle where his stomach bulged. His face was greasy and pitted. He passed behind the counter and without a word to the girl went through to the kitchen. In a couple of minutes he was back wearing a grubby white coat.

'All right, Julie, buzz off.'

She showed him her bill-pad.

'Okay.'

She, in turn, went through to the kitchen and came back a little later wearing a brown coat which fitted her figure and an orange scarf. Milton followed her out, feeling that the eyes of everybody in the café were on him.

'Was that the owner?'

'Yes.'

'He looks a rough sort of chap.'

'He's all right.'

He was to realise that Julie rarely spoke with warm approval of anybody but neither did she condemn.

She added after a moment, 'He owns four other cafés in the town and he races whippets.'

As they set out down Commercial Road she took his arm just as if they were an old married couple.

'Julie, I ought to tell you—'

'You don't have to tell me anything. What I want to know, I'll ask. Okay?'

'Okay.'

They turned up Canal Street and she pushed open the door of number twenty-one.

'It's me!'

He followed her upstairs.

'I'll have to change. If you want to clean your shoes go downstairs and right through to the back kitchen.'

He went down again, through the passage, past the sitting room where the television was on. There was a door at the end of the passage and he knocked, but there was no answer so he opened it. A kitchen with a cooker, a refrigerator, a large plastic-topped table and a sink. Beyond the kitchen there was a lean-to and there, on one of the shelves, he found shoe-cleaning materials. While he was standing in his socks, cleaning his shoes, the landlady came through into the kitchen.

'Oh, it's you.'

'I hope you don't mind.'

'My dear man! Make yourself at home, that's the way.'

She filled a kettle and put it on the gas. 'By the way, I hope we didn't disturb you last night?'

'What? No....'

'Charlie and me has been friends from way back.' She reached down the tea-caddy. 'I'm making a cup of tea if you'd like one.'

'Thank you.'

'Charlie's married, of course, lives up in Carlisle, three kids, but when he's down this way he treats this like a second home.'

He drank his tea, thanked her and went upstairs in his stockinged feet. He heard water running in the bathroom and guessed that it was Julie, so he went in his bedroom to wait.

A few minutes later she came into his room, wearing her wrap. 'You've done your shoes? What about your trousers? Have you got a clothes brush?'

'No, I'm sorry.'

'All right, give them to me, you can't go out like that.'

It was astounding; he was behaving like a little boy with his mother. He slipped down his trousers and handed them to her.

'All right, I'll do them while you're in the bathroom.'

He was fascinated by this new world in which he found himself. It seemed so incredibly uncomplicated. He tried to think of a word which described the attitudes of Julie and her mother and he could think of only one—*acceptance*. People are what they are; events are what they are....

Julie was very little older than the sixth form girls he taught, very little older than Elizabeth, yet he could not feel that she needed to be protected or shielded. If anything it was he who felt conscious of his inexperience, of a certain naivety.

'All right, I'm ready.'

She was wearing the same brown coat, but under it she had on a tartan skirt and a white, terylene jumper with a polo neck.

He followed her down the stairs.

'I'm off, mum.'

Her mother came to the door of the sitting room. She saw Milton and looked mildly surprised. 'Oh, so that's how it is.'

Julie slammed the door behind them.

'Do you think your mother minds?'

'Why should she?'

They were crossing the green to the bus stop and the wind blew tiny flakes of wet sleet into their faces.

'Do you like Indian food?'

'I don't think I've ever had any.'

'Curry.'

'Oh, I like curry if it's not too hot.'

They went to an Indian restaurant in the Grove and they had a table for two. In the dim light her hair shone and her white jumper emphasised her youth and gave her an air of unassailable innocence. She liked the little dishes of chutney, chopped onion and coconut and she was intrigued by the popadums, of which she ate two.

The restaurant was filling up and he looked a little anxiously at each group of newcomers in case there was someone he knew, but people who saw them must have thought they were father and daughter. They looked, he thought, quite ordinary and nobody could suspect the wild chaos of his mind. It was not unpleasant, like being on some sort of roller-coaster; he had spent the day in a slow agonizing ascent to a summit, now he was on the breath-taking downward run, out of control. It astonished him to hear his own voice, which sounded, as usual, dry and calm.

'Do you like it?'

'It's very nice. Different from the café.'

The waiter helped them on with their coats. 'Good night, sir. Good night, miss.'

There were only two major cinemas left in the city; the others were small and catered for a specialised clientele. They chose the Plaza. The main film, set in Berlin, concerned two double agents, one a seductive blonde, the other a red-blooded American male. It took ninety minutes for them to discover that they were both on the same side and to climb into the same bed.

In one of the more exciting sequences she reached out and gripped his hand and continued to hold it. Finally he put his arm round her and she relaxed against him.

One Saturday afternoon, with youthful enthusiasm, he had taken the sixth form history set to the city museum where, by prior arrangement, they were shown documents concerning the late eighteenth and early nineteenth century history of the city. Christine was among them, taking notes and asking questions. Afterwards when they were coming down the steps from the museum, he said:

'Well, I'll leave you all to find your own way home. I hope you enjoyed it.'

'Oh, yes, it was great ... Thanks for arranging it, Mr Milton....'

When the others had gone she was still there, standing on the steps in her dark-blue gaberdine raincoat, her fair hair more curly than usual because of the misty rain.

'Going home, Mr Milton?'

'I'm in digs, worse luck. I thought of going to a café for some tea.'

Her solemn eyes met his.

'Would you like to have tea with me, Christine? Or are your parents expecting you home?'

'No, mother's gone to see her sister and father's on two-till-ten shift.'

The tea shop was above a bakery.

'Aren't you going to take your mack off?'

He had helped her off with her mackintosh and hung it on the bent-wood stand. Somehow this simple act had taken on a special significance. Until that moment he had only seen her in her school uniform; now she wore a close-fitting woollen dress which emphasised her breasts and made her look older. She no longer looked like a schoolgirl and he felt shy.

They sat at a table by the window and they were level with people on the top decks of passing buses. She ate cream cakes with a fork, leaving her plate and her fingers clean, while he had cream all over the place.

'What is your first name?'

'Arthur, I'm afraid.'

'I think it's a nice name, may I call you by it?'

He blushed. 'I suppose it's all right when we're off duty, so to speak.'

They finished their tea and he helped her on with her coat; then they went out into the street, where it was still drizzling rain. A little way along they came to the Plaza Cinema which was showing *The Seven Samurai* and they stopped to look at the stills outside.

'Have you seen it?'

'No.' He was lying.

'They say it's very good.'

'Would you like to go?'

'Could we?'

He took tickets for the most expensive seats and sat at the back because he thought they were less likely to be seen. Half-way through the film she put her hand over his, and a little later she guided his arm round her shoulders. Her head rested against him and her hair tickled his cheek. Greatly daring he kissed her hair and she raised her lips to him. He was intoxicated.

That had been the beginning.

At half past five Symons reported by telephone and Hammond cross-questioned him.

'The *Chronicle* offices, what did he want there?'

'According to the girl on the counter he wanted to refer to some of their back numbers. He asked for the volume covering the second half of 1956.'

'Does 1956 count as history?'

'I dunno, sarge; why?'

'Well, that's what he teaches, isn't it?' Hammond yawned. 'How long did he spend talking to his wife?'

'Two or three minutes. I've no idea what they talked about but it seemed to me that he gave her the brush-off.'

'And you say he's staying with Nellie Grace in Canal Street.'

'Do you know her, sarge?'

'Who doesn't? She used to be on the game until a few years ago, when she came into a bit of money and set up that lodging house business. Now she's come all over respectable and gives out that she's a widow. But she's a widow that was never married.'

'Married or not, she's got a daughter who works in the café on the green.'

'I know.'

'Well, Milton picked the girl up there and they went home together, arm-in-arm.'

'I'll be damned! I didn't think he was that sort. How do you know that he's actually lodging with Nellie?'

'After they went in I called on Nellie and pretended to be interested in somebody called Parsons. She said she hadn't got a lodger called Parsons. At the moment she'd only got three lorry drivers who'd been coming there for years and, wait for it, a Mr Stuart.'

'Stuart?'

'That's what she said. I asked her if it was Mr Stuart who had just come in with her daughter and she said it was.'

'So Milton's changed his name. I wonder why?'

'It's suspicious, sarge, when you take it along with the rest. We've more than enough to bring him in for questioning.'

Hammond was emphatic. 'Not on your life! The brass are losing interest in Milton; they've found other fish to fry.'

'Something new?'

'I can't tell you over the phone. Where are you now?'

'In a phone box at the end of Canal Street. I can still see the house.'

Hammond hesitated.

'Do you want me to pack it in?'

'No, stay where you are and I'll send somebody to relieve you.'

Chapter Seven

THAT NIGHT HE was less disturbed by his landlady and her lover; either they were more circumspect or he was more detached. He woke at seven, washed and dressed and had his breakfast, then returned to his room. It was another cold day, and he watched the postman leaning against the bitter wind as he made his way along the street. He sat by the gas fire feeling slack and empty, the new exercise book open on his knees.

He wrote at the top of the first page: 'Tuesday November 9th'. He intended to write an account of the previous day, but the more he thought about it the more clearly he realised that he could not separate the thoughts and events of that day from what had gone before. If the record was to have any justification it must trace the reasons for his conduct, step by step, clearly and logically. Otherwise it would be like starting a serial story in the middle. The task dismayed him and he sat for a long time staring at the fire, vaguely aware of the sounds of life going on around him. He heard the whine of the electric motor on the milk-float, the clink of bottles, doors slamming, the occasional 'ping' of the door-bell at the shop on the corner.

In the end he wrote one word: 'Christine'; and a little later he added another—'Julie'. At one point he seemed about to write something else, but he changed his mind and closed the book.

He got out his travelling case from the bottom of the wardrobe, unlocked it and put the book inside. Then he searched amongst the clothing he had not unpacked until he found a grey envelope, the envelope which contained Christine's photograph and the five letters she had written to him. They were all on pale blue, lined paper in a round, childish hand:

'Dearest Arthur,
    I am coming to see you on Sunday ...'

He finished his term of student teaching at Atherton Road towards the end of March and went home for the Easter vacation. He had one more term to do in college for his diploma then, all being well, he would be starting his first job. It was when he returned to his lodgings in mid-April that he received his first letter from Christine. She announced that she was coming to see him on the following Sunday and wanted him to meet her at the coach station.

The letter came as a shock. Although there had been no doubt of his tender feeling for her during those days in March, he had thought about her very little since and had returned to college deeply preoccupied with the need to get a good final assessment and a job. Common sense as well as conscience counselled against a clandestine involvement with a school-girl.

Sunday was one of those April days which go a long way to compensate for a cold, wet and dreary winter. The sun shone, the air was suffused with golden light, the trees in the park were decked out in fresh lime-green and it was warm enough to go without a coat. Her coach was due in at half past ten, and he was there a quarter of an hour early. He would talk to her kindly and sensibly; he would make her see that any relationship was impossible.

The coach came in. There were not many people on it and, by chance, she was the last one off. All he saw was that she wore a light-blue coat and that she was smiling. Then she was in his arms and he had lifted her off her feet, kissing her hair, her eyes, her lips and the tip of her nose.

She came on four Sundays during that term and it was as though events had conspired to smooth their path. His land-lady, an elderly widow, visited her sister on Sundays, and they could count on having the house to themselves until six or seven in the evening. On Christine's second visit the day was grey and overcast with frequent showers. They went to a café for lunch but returned to his bed-sitter afterwards. It was a gloomy little room looking out on a brick wall. They sat in front of the gas fire; he had the threadbare armchair while she sat on the hearth-rug, resting against his knees. He went down to the kitchen to make some coffee and when he came back she was still seated on the hearth-rug, but now she was naked, her body lit by the orange glow of the fire.

It was the first time that he had made love, but though he did not realise it at the time, she was not a virgin.

At the coach-station he said, 'Now that we know we really love each other, dear, there is no need to be secretive. After all, there isn't that much difference in our ages. Of course, we shall have to wait a year or two, but if you explain all that to your parents....'

She looked up at him, put a finger on his lips and whispered. 'This is our secret; why tell people?'

It was the first time in twenty years that he had faced the memory of that day and he felt a sense of wonderment that such a thing should have happened to him. It made him intensely sad, though at that moment he could not have said why. For a time he stood by the window looking down into the street. He was having difficulty getting back; it was like waking from a compelling dream, and he was half inclined to believe that was what it had been.

He put on his coat, tucked a warm muffler round his neck and let himself out into the street. He walked to Commercial Road and up to the green. For once the windows of the café were clear of steam and he could see Julie, leaning on the counter, apparently reading. The police caravan at the entrance to the park looked deserted. He glanced up at the flats and wondered if Jean was looking out of one of the windows.

There was a telephone kiosk near the bus stop and he went in, looked up a number and dialled the Central Police Station.

'Police.'

'May I speak to Chief Inspector Welsh, please?'

'Chief Inspector Welsh? He retired years ago. Who's speaking?'

'I want to get in touch with him, it's a personal matter. I wonder if you could give me his address?'

A moment of hesitation. 'We are not allowed to give addresses. If you will tell me who you are....'

He dropped the receiver. It was no surprise to hear that Welsh had retired, but at least he had confirmed the fact. He turned again to the telephone directory. There were eighteen

Welshes listed, four with the initial 'J', but one of these was a dental surgeon. Of the remaining three, two lived in suburban areas which might be considered suitable for retirement. He dialled the first.

'464342.' A woman's voice.

'I want to speak to ex-Chief Inspector John Welsh.'

'I'm sorry, but you must have the wrong Welsh.'

He tried the second number.

'Mrs Welsh speaking.'

'I want to speak to ex-Chief Inspector—'

'I'm sorry, my husband passed away last July.'

An unexpected setback. For the moment he could not think what to do. He bought a paper and caught a bus which would pass through the city centre. A minor headline in the newspaper caught his eye:

TOW-PATH MURDER
DEVELOPMENTS EXPECTED

Police investigating the murder of Mr Kenneth Jobling, whose body was found on the tow-path in Commercial Road on Saturday, are believed to have established a connection between this and another major crime. In an interview late last night Detective Chief Superintendent Goddard would neither confirm nor deny the report, but he said that in his opinion an arrest would not be long delayed.

'Another major crime'—what did it mean? Milton was puzzled and concerned.

He was sitting on one of the cross-seats on the lower deck of the bus and he was aware of someone watching him. He lowered his paper and met the eyes of a young man sitting opposite, across the gangway. The man dropped his eyes at once. He was fair and very tall. Milton thought that his face was familiar but could not place him. Perhaps he was a parent of a pupil at the school, but he seemed too young for that.

When Milton got off at the city centre, the young man was behind him.

He needed money and he decided to draw thirty pounds from the city branch of his bank, using his banker's card, rather than go to his own branch where they might show some interest in his welfare. The cashier paid over the money without question and as he came out of the bank he saw the young man again, looking in a shop window not thirty yards away.

He was being followed!

He had just remembered where he had seen the man before; he was the constable who had accompanied Sergeant Hammond. Evidently they did not care whether or not he knew that he was under observation. At first he was greatly perturbed, but then it occurred to him that if they had a case against him he would have been taken into custody before now.

It was bitterly cold, the sky was leaden, and it seemed inevitable that there would be snow before night-fall. He felt the need of hot food and went to a restaurant patronised by people who worked nearby. The meal was reasonable but the place was so crowded that he had scarcely room to move his elbows. Everybody seemed to know everybody else and he felt as though he had gate-crashed a family party.

He had made up his mind on the next step now that he was unable to talk to ex-Chief Inspector Welsh. He would pay another visit to Christine's mother. It was only a quarter to two and he wanted to arrive in the middle of the afternoon, when they would have finished lunch but there would still be time to talk before the boy arrived home from school. To pass the time he went to the public library. The magazine room was popular on such a cold day but he found a chair and, for form's sake, a magazine. It was a periodical for bird fanciers and might as well have been written in Sanskrit. He had not been there long before he saw his shadow peering through the glass door. Their eyes met briefly and the man withdrew.

The room was very warm, which made him drowsy, and he caught himself drifting off.

'Hurt me, Arthur! ... Hurt me! ... I *want* you to....'

He tried to suppress the recollection but could not. It was only the second time they had made love and it came to him as a revelation. He could scarcely recognize her; her white distorted face, her drawn lips, the convulsive movements of her

106

head and the cries which issued through her clenched teeth. She clung to him as though she were drowning; her nails sank into his flesh and her breathing frightened him.

But ten minutes later she was sitting up, calmly examining marks on her thigh. 'You did that,' she said, and she was smiling at him as though in gratitude for some special tenderness.

Incredible!

He had learned a great deal, and not least about himself. There was that within him which responded to her needs and her demands. He had had to exercise great self-control. Was it possible that she had intuitively recognised in him latent needs and desires which were the complement of her own? Had she also believed that his timidity and natural caution would be a kind of safety net?

Mrs Wilson smoothed the green tablecloth. She was puzzled by Milton's second visit and a little embarrassed by it. It was evident that she had heard rumours and, no doubt, Elizabeth had talked to Alan. It occurred to him with something of a shock that Elizabeth might be a regular visitor to this very room.

Mrs Wilson's sister, Joyce, sat by the fire, her arms resting limply on the arms of her chair. Her skin had lost all its colour and the only sign of vitality in her whole body came when she spoke. Even then her speech was slow and seemed to cost her a great effort.

Milton had planned what he would say: 'I've really come because I think I owe you and Alan an apology. I feel that I've treated the boy badly, but I expect you know that I've had a very difficult time recently.'

'Alan tells us very little, but he did say that you were away from school. You don't have to apologise, Mr Milton; troubles come to us, we don't choose them.'

'Make a cup of tea, Janie.' The invalid turned to Milton with a faint smile. 'I expect Mr Milton could do with a cup of tea, it's a bitter day.'

The room, in fact, was uncomfortably hot and Milton was conscious of that oppressive aura which surrounds the chronically sick.

'Don't make tea on my account.'

107

'We always have a cup at about this time.'

Mrs Wilson went out into the kitchen and left him with her sister. They were silent for a while, listening to the sound of the kettle being filled and the plop of the gas being lit.

'I've seen you looking at the photograph.'

Milton did not know what to say, so he said nothing.

She was overcome by a fit of coughing. When she had recovered, she went on, 'Alan is the image of her; he should have been a girl, looks like that are wasted on a boy.'

Milton murmured something agreeable.

'She'd be thirty-seven or eight if she was alive today.'

The room was so dimly lit by the cold, afternoon light that he had difficulty in seeing the picture clearly.

Mrs Wilson came in with the tray. She placed it on the table and set about pouring tea.

'I was telling Mr Milton about Christine.'

'Sugar, Mr Milton?'

She passed him a cup and poured one for her sister, then she glanced up at the photograph.

'Twenty years ago; sometimes it seems only yesterday. She was murdered, you know—strangled.'

She spoke with that brutal frankness which is sometimes characteristic of people who have suffered and learned to live with suffering.

'A girl of seventeen, never harmed a soul. We'd been on holiday in Weston, my husband and me, and we'd left Chris at home. When we got back we found her, they said she'd been dead for more than twenty-four hours....'

She took a rolled-up handkerchief from the pocket of her cardigan and dabbed her eyes.

'Don't upset yourself, Janie.'

She shook her head. 'It does me good to talk about it now and then. Better than keeping it all bottled up inside.' She sipped her tea. 'What sort of man would do a thing like that? I'll never forgive myself for letting her stay in the house alone, but she wanted to. You know what girls are like at that age; going off with mum and dad on holiday isn't their idea of fun any longer.'

Milton felt that he must say something. 'They never found him—the man who... ?'

108

'No. That ... that *beast* is still going about among decent people.'

'The police did their best, Janie.'

She put her cup down and resumed stroking the tablecloth. 'Yes, I've nothing but good to say of what they did. They tried. That inspector—Welsh, his name was—he couldn't have done more if she'd been his own daughter. And Sergeant Tabb—Tabby, we used to call him—he was almost like one of the family. Still never a Christmas goes by without a card. Of course, he's finished with the police force now—packed it in and gone farming over to Laker. His people were farmers....'

She got up again and went out of the room. A minute or two later she was back with a photograph album, which she opened on the table in front of him.

'That's Jim, my husband.'

It was a photograph of about a dozen men, all in tunics with shining buttons and all clutching brass-band instruments.

'Jim was thirty-five or six then.'

A tall, fair man with a thin moustache, he held his trombone and looked at the camera with an air of embarrassment.

'They formed the band between them and they used to play in the streets on Saturday morning, collecting for charity.' She sighed. 'They were good days.'

Her slender forefinger hovered once more over the photograph. 'That's Tabby with the cornet. He was in the band, that's how we came to know him. Of course he was younger than Jim, several years younger ... Tabby was in the uniformed force then; that was before he went into C.I.D.'

Joyce said: 'They had a squad of men on it for more than four months but they didn't get anywhere.'

'Nowhere at all. Tabby reckoned it must have been a stranger, somebody from away, but why would she let such a man into the house?'

Milton had scarcely touched his tea; he could not trust himself to raise the cup to his lips.

Mrs Wilson went on: 'What I can't understand is why the neighbours didn't see anything. Of course, it was the second week in August, all the factories closed and the town more than half empty.'

Outside the window the air was full of white flakes drifting down. The snow had come.

He arrived by coach at mid-day, one of no more than a dozen passengers. The coach station, under its vast roof, was dimly lit and pleasantly cool, but as he came out on to the forecourt the sudden glare almost blinded him and the melting tarmac stuck to the soles of his shoes. He went to a refreshment kiosk and drank two glasses of chilled fruit drink. The girl who served him did not speak and scarcely bothered to look in his direction. Although she wore a brief, sleeveless frock, there were patches of sweat beneath her arms.

The town was like a ghost town; it was easy to imagine that it had been evacuated in the face of some imminent but invisible peril. Most of the shops had 'closed' notices and those which were open appeared to be empty.

It was two miles to Bewdley Street, but there was no direct bus route and he would have thought it a gross extravagance to take a taxi, so he walked, keeping where possible in the shade of the buildings. He wore a white shirt open at the neck and blue drill trousers and carried a haversack slung over his shoulder. He must have looked a gawky youth with his long, thin body.

Christine had written:

Dearest,
  I have fixed it so that I shall be in the house alone all the week while dad and mum are in Weston. . . .

But he had a vacation job, and though he asked for time off he was refused. As he couldn't afford to be independent he had to wait for his day off. He knew that she would be disappointed and guessed that she would be angry, but there was nothing he could do.

He knew the city well enough to take short cuts, avoiding the city centre, but they took him through an industrial district where the roads were lined with high, chain-link fences and there was no shade. His head began to ache. He

110

arrived at last at the junction with Atherton Road, just below the school, and he turned right down Bewdley Street. In those days the street had a well-cared-for look; in many cases the red brick had been cleaned and pointed, the woodwork painted in bright colours and the little gardens cultivated, so that each house had individuality.

Number sixteen had the pointed brickwork picked out in white, the windows and door were lime-green and the brass door-knob and letter-box were brilliantly polished. Photographs of it would soon be in all the newspapers and Bewdley Street would have its moment of notoriety.

He was unsure of his reception and though he longed to see her and to hold her in his arms he could not still a nagging anxiety.

'You haven't touched your tea!'

He made apologetic noises.

'It's my fault, running on about my troubles, but it's good to have somebody to talk to now and then, somebody who understands. You've got a teen-aged daughter so you can have some idea of what I went through. You give them your love, you care for them and bring them up decently then some man ... some *animal*. ...'

He escaped. Outside the street was carpeted with snow and it was still falling, dense, purposeful and silent. He was almost overwhelmed by emotion and he walked in a dream, fighting to control his features and to avoid bursting into tears. For what? For whom?

'*I'm afraid.*'

'*What are you afraid of?*'

'*Of guilt.*'

'*Of what are you guilty?*'

'*I'm not sure.*'

It was only while he was waiting at the bus-stop that he remembered his shadow and saw the young man, hatless, his coat collar turned up, plodding down the street towards him. He caught a bus to the city centre then another to the green. He wanted to see Julie.

The park was transformed; every bough and every twig was outlined in snow. Lights sparkled everywhere and seemed twice as bright as usual; even the window of the café was

111

crystal clear. By the park-gate a Land Rover was backing up to the police caravan as though to take it in tow, and he was surprised by his lack of interest.

Julie was his only link now.

Link with what? Not with the past, certainly. Perhaps with the present, with reality. He could look across to the flats where his wife and daughter were living and feel nothing. The school was no more than an incident in his life; it had left no enduring impression. His house, his car, his books might have belonged to somebody else. He was utterly lacking in any feeling of attachment or possession towards them. He was a man without ties, a man whose past seemed to be concentrated—focused—on that lime-green door with the brass letter-box and door-knob.

He pushed open the door of the café with a tremor of anticipation but was immediately disappointed. It was not Julie behind the counter, but the fat man with the pock-marked face and dirty white coat. Milton stood, holding the door open and the man turned towards him.

'Make up your mind, mister, it's like a perishing ice-box with that door open.'

'I was looking for Julie.'

'It's her half-day.'

Hammond came into his office, stamping his feet to restore the circulation.

'Well?'

'I'm typing my report, sarge.'

'I can see that, but what happened?'

'I've heard through the grape-vine that the Jobling case is wrapped up.'

'For once, you've heard right. Isles, Jobling's partner, and two other men have been charged with the murder, and it won't be long before they're also charged with a string of art robberies. Isles was using his inside knowledge, obtained through the office, to master-mind these break-ins. Apparently Jobling tumbled to it and thereby hangs the tale.'

'So Fido is off the hook?'

'If by Fido you mean Milton, yes.'

'So I don't have to tail him.'

'Yes, you do.'

'But if the case is all over bar the shouting, where does he come in?'

'He doesn't, not in the Jobling case, but look at it this way: three weeks ago Fido's wife left him to go to live with Jobling. Next day Fido was round there doing his best to cause a breach of the peace and a fortnight later Jobling was murdered.

'Naturally we went after the wronged husband. He did his best to lead us up the garden path by saying that he wasn't in the neighbourhood of Commercial Road when the crime was committed. We were able to prove different, so what does he do? He walks out of his job, leaves his house, and goes to some doss house in Canal Street where he lives under an assumed name.'

Hammond paused and glared at his subordinate. 'Doesn't that strike you as odd?'

'All right, he's a nutter, but if we know he isn't guilty. . . .'

'All we know is that he's not guilty of slugging the insurance man. But he's done something and I'd like to know what.'

Symons nodded. 'I see.'

'I'm glad. Now perhaps you'll answer my question. What's he been up to?'

'Well, he left the house at about 10.45 this morning and walked to the green.'

'To the café?'

'No, he went to a call-box by the bus stop and made two or three calls.'

'Got any numbers?'

'I got there just as he was putting the receiver down after his first call. I think the second was a wrong number because he only said one or two words.' Symons looked at his notes. 'But I got the third. The number he called was 476481.'

'Have you checked it?'

'I haven't had a minute, sarge, not within range of a phone until now.'

Hammond picked up the telephone and asked for directory enquiries.

'Central Police Station, Detective Sergeant Hammond. I'd be grateful for the name and address of the subscriber whose

113

number is 476481 ... Thanks, I've got that.'

He replaced the receiver. 'John Welsh, 52, Merton Drive, Edgington.'

Symons looked blank.

'Ex-Detective Chief Inspector John Welsh.'

'I thought he was dead.'

'He is, but Fido may not have known that.'

Hammond hesitated, then picked up the phone again and dialled a number. His conversation was very brief.

'That was Welsh's wife. Milton asked for Welsh and she told him that her husband had passed away, so he rang off.'

'I still don't see....'

'Never mind, get on with your story.'

'Well, he bought a paper and got a bus to the centre. He went into a bank and came out putting notes in his wallet. He had lunch in a place called "The Full Platter", then he spent half-an-hour in the magazine room of the library snoozing. After that he walked to Gordon Street and went into Farley House—that's one of the new blocks of flats. I was close behind him and I saw from the indicator that he'd got out of the lift on the fifth. I didn't know which flat he'd gone into so I nipped up to the fifth and waited. After about an hour he came out of Flat G. While I was waiting I'd briefed myself on the occupants and G belongs to a Mr and Mrs Sparkes.'

'Then?'

'I followed him to the café in the green and eventually back to Canal Street where, I hope to God, he stays.'

Hammond frowned. 'I think I'd better have a word with the brass about this.'

'Do I carry on tomorrow?'

'Unless I tell you different.'

Chapter Eight

THERE WERE FOUR others at breakfast on Thursday morning but the landlady's special friend, Charlie, had left before six on his way back to Carlisle. All were on first-name terms with each other and with the landlady, so that Milton was conscious of being odd man out. When the landlady addressed him as Mr Stuart he was aware of their amused glances. The radio was on, broadcasting a local progamme interspersed with news items.

After a weather report which claimed that the city was experiencing the most severe November weather in sixty years, the news-reader went on:

'The tow-path murder: news has just come in that Geoffrey Isles and two other men have been jointly charged with the murder of Kenneth Jobling, the city insurance consultant. Isles was a junior partner in the dead man's firm. The other men charged are Jack Roper, a car-spares dealer of Commercial Road, and Ernest Wilder, an antique dealer of Westover.

'It is expected that further charges will be brought against the three men in connection with a series of burglaries in which antiques and works of art worth more than £50,000 were stolen. It is believed that information obtained through the office of the deceased was used to plan and execute the burglaries. Detective Chief Superintendent Goddard, who is in charge of the case, said that he wished to make it clear that there is no evidence to suggest that Mr Jobling was involved in the crimes.'

Milton listened to the news with scarcely a tremor of interest.

It was no longer snowing, but the sky was overcast and there was a bitter wind. The streets had been cleared but elsewhere the snow remained. He had no need to look up Sergeant Tabb in the telephone book, for Laker was only a tiny village a few miles from the city and there would be no difficulty in finding him.

He walked up Commercial Road to the green, noted that he was being followed by the same young man as on the previous day and for the first time felt irritated by the surveillance. He decided to shake the man off and, to his surprise, he succeeded very easily. By glancing back at frequent intervals he eventually saw a cruising taxi which would soon overtake him. He waited for the taxi to draw almost level, then signalled to the driver. The taxi pulled up some yards ahead. Milton ran after it, jumped in and slammed the door.

'Laker village.'

He paid off the taxi in the village square, which had a pub on one side and a rather ugly Victorian church on the other. Although it was mid-morning there was no one about; the wind whistled down from the hills and every now and then flurries of snow or sleet swept over the village like a billowing curtain. He crossed the square to a little shop by the pub, his shoes squeaking in the dry snow.

'Tabb? That's the ex-policeman. He lives up at "Keston", it's a small farm. You go up the lane by the pub and you come to a place surrounded by pine trees, that's "Keston".'

The lane was steep, creased with frost-hardened ridges, and it seemed to run straight up into the hills. Milton could see sheep on the lower slopes but the peaks were lost in blue-black clouds. 'Keston', when he found it was surrounded, not by pine trees, but by a massive weather-guard of *Cupressus* which were stooping to the wind.

Within their protective screen it was comparatively calm. He found himself in a yard with a house on one side and outbuildings on two others. In one of the outbuildings a man was working, a big man with close-cropped hair. He wore a blue jersey and corduroy trousers and he was a few years older than Milton.

'Mr Tabb?'

'That's me.'

The ex-detective was working on the engine of a small tractor.

'I wonder if I might have a word with you?'

'What about?'

He did not look up from the machine and Milton was not encouraged. He had prepared his story but he was nervous.

116

'My name is Stuart, Charles Stuart. I write crime stories—detective novels.'

'I'm afraid I never read 'em, I've had too much of the real thing.'

'That's the point really, I want to pick your brains.'

'Oh?' The massive fingers still fiddled with a tiny screw and his tone lacked any warmth or interest.

'I want to do a book based on the Christine Wilson case.'

Tabb said nothing for a long time; he succeeded in catching the thread on his screw and tightened it in position. 'I'm not sure that I would like that.' He finally straightened up and faced Milton. 'In any case, I can't tell you anything that wasn't in the papers.'

'I think you can. I want to know how the police set about a case of that sort, the nature and scope of the investigation.'

Tabb was wiping his hands on a piece of rag. 'I see. I suppose there's no harm in talking.'

'I'd be very grateful for anything you felt able to tell me.'

Milton thought that he handled Tabb rather well and it had turned out to be easier than he had expected. He had always supposed that being an imposter must be difficult.

'You'd better come inside.'

Tabb was a slow-moving giant. He had a large, expressive face, the colour of tanned leather. He led the way into the living room of the house. There was a good fire in an open grate, the matting was dusty with dried soil, the furniture had a well-used look and an open roll-topped desk was littered with papers. A wall-clock with a shining brass pendulum ticked away over the fireplace.

'Let's have your coat.'

Tabb took it and threw it across the back of the settee. 'Beer or coffee?'

'A cup of coffee would be very pleasant.'

'I'll tell the wife.'

He went into the back premises, returned after a minute or two and sat in the armchair on the other side of the fire from Milton. His steady gaze was disquieting.

'You're quite sure you're not a muck-raking journalist?'

'No, I'm not a journalist. I have no connection with newspapers.'

'Anyway, I'm afraid you're going to be disappointed. There isn't much to tell. After all, we didn't get anywhere, did we?'

'But that wasn't for the want of trying.'

'No, you're right, we did our best.'

It was soon apparent that despite his reservations Tabb was not unwilling to talk.

'I wasn't on the case at the start. I'd been sent off on a course and I didn't get back until the investigation had been going for a week. On the face of it you'd have said it was a straight-forward case. I know that John Welsh expected to have it all wrapped up in a few days but, as it turned out we were no further forward after four months and then, as they say, active enquiries were suspended.

'You see, there was evidence to show that the chap, whoever he was, had been in the house for several hours before he killed her. But he wasn't holding her prisoner or anything like that; she was up at the corner shop during that Saturday morning, buying this and that. We found a meal laid for two people on the kitchen table.'

'It must have been someone she knew well.' Milton felt bound to say something though he would have preferred to remain silent.

'That's what we thought, but it didn't get us anywhere. We collected several of the chap's hairs, we got his blood-group from the seminal fluid but no finger prints and nobody had seen him.

'As a rule, all you've got to do in a case like that is to go through the girl's male acquaintances until you find the one that fits. . . .'

Tabb paused, studying the dirt in his finger nails and picking away at it.

'After all, she wasn't a young tart; in fact, most of the people who knew her thought that she was unusually quiet. One or two of her girl friends had a different view, but even they thought it was unlikely that she had ever let a boy take her to bed. Of course, they were wrong about that.'

Mrs Tabb brought in the coffee. She was a tall, big-boned woman and she had little to say for herself. Without being rude she made it clear that her husband's acquaintances were no concern of hers. She acknowledged Tabb's introduction and went back to her kitchen where, to judge by the smell, she was preparing some sort of savoury stew.

Tabb sipped his coffee, made a face and added more sugar. Milton tried to prompt him. 'Isn't it odd that the neighbours didn't see anything?'

Tabb nodded. 'You'd think so. But there are two things to be remembered: first, it was holiday week and many of the houses in the street were empty; second, these people live in their kitchens not their front rooms. Anyway, nobody did see anything, or if they did they didn't tell us about it. One woman, living opposite to the Wilsons, reckoned she'd heard somebody go in there in the early hours of Saturday morning but that was all. She didn't get out of bed to look.'

Tabb finished his coffee. 'Want some more?'

'No, thank you.'

A sudden squall of wind rattled the window sashes and caused the fire to puff out smoke.

Tabb shrugged. 'It's rough here now but it's a grand place in the summer.' He put an extra log on the fire.

'As I was saying, we questioned the neighbours and got nowhere; we interviewed every male member of the school over the age of fourteen, including the staff. We talked to all the girls of about her age and got nothing that led anywhere. Then we cast the net wider and checked every male who was likely to have had any sort of contact with her, including the baker, the milkman, the coalman, the postman and the kid who delivered newspapers to the house. There was strong local feeling; the Wilsons were well known and liked, so we had plenty of co-operation. At the finish we had collected over fifteen hundred statements, almost all of them quite useless.

'Of course, we were driven to the conclusion that the man was a stranger to the district. That got us nowhere either, for we had already checked the railway stations and coach and bus termini as a matter of routine.'

Tabb stopped and picked up a smouldering ember from the hearth and threw it back in the fire.

'We had only one lead. The girl's mother told us that in recent months Christine had spent the odd Sunday with a certain girl friend. When we questioned the girl it turned out that Christine had not been with her on any of the

119

Sundays in question. Well, where had she been? Of course, we didn't find the answer to that one either.'

He sighed. 'Four months work and nothing at the end of it.'

They were silent while an aircraft flew over, very low.

'You'd think those things would be grounded this weather.'

Outside it was getting darker and another snow-fall seemed imminent. Milton began to feel concerned about getting back but, as yet, he had learned very little from his visit. Now the detective leaned forward and adopted a more confidential manner.

'I wouldn't like this to go any further; we didn't give it to the press. As you know, she was strangled, but her body carried other signs of injury, nothing very serious—bruises, teeth-marks—you understand?'

Milton agreed bleakly.

'The pathologist said that these injuries had been inflicted shortly before death, but there were others, similar in kind, which were much fainter and at least a month older. You see what I mean?'

Milton nodded, not trusting himself to speak.

Tabb sighed. 'In a way, it makes what happened more credible, more understandable, don't you think?'

Tabb bent down and poked the fire vigorously until the sparks flew up the chimney.

It was an effort for Milton to sustain the rôle in which he had cast himself.

'I can understand how you felt. I heard that you were a friend of the family.'

'Who told you that?' Tabb snapped out the words.

Milton was surprised and confused by the sudden aggression but he kept his head.

'I can't remember, I have talked to several people about the case. Why? Wasn't it true?'

Tabb dropped the poker in the fender and sat back in his chair. 'I was never a friend of the family. I knew her father because we played in the same brass band; there was no other connection—none.'

For some reason he was disturbed and it was some time before he spoke again. When he did it was with great deliberation:

'You didn't need to be a friend of the family to be upset by the girl's death and the way she died. I was still young enough to be impressionable—not yet case-hardened. But I think anybody who saw that girl lying there, naked, on the bed, would have felt as I felt.'

Milton could recall the room in photographic detail. The double-bed took up most of the space but there was a dressing-table with a swing mirror and a cane chair which had been painted blue and sprayed with gold. The room was dimly lit from a window on the left over which curtains must have been drawn. A blue eiderdown and other bedclothes were heaped at the foot of the bed while Christine lay on her back, her legs slightly bent. She was naked. Her eyes stared at the ceiling, expressionless and unusually prominent; her face was swollen and suffused with colour; her lips were parted in an agonised rictus and there were marks on her throat and on her arms and thighs. A little foam had gathered at the corners of her mouth.

He knew that he was going to be sick and almost tumbled down the stairs and into the kitchen, where he vomited in the sink. He rinsed out the sink and stood, supporting himself against it until he felt more settled. He tried breathing deeply and gradually acquired a better control of his nerves. He was tempted to go out through the back, but he realised that he might run a greater risk of being seen, so he returned to the little hall and stood for a moment at the bottom of the stairs listening. The silence was complete.

He opened the front door and was almost blinded by the brilliance of the sunshine. He looked up and down the street. It was deserted and, as quietly as possible, he closed the door behind him.

Tabb was looking at him with a curious expression.

'I'm sorry. I must have been day-dreaming.'

But Tabb's gaze did not waver and Milton felt sure that he was becoming suspicious. He made a great effort to recover his composure.

'I must be getting back, it was very good of you to spare me so much of your time....' He stood up and picked up his coat from the settee.

Tabb did not attempt to detain him but glanced at the clock over the fireplace.

'There's a bus from the square in twenty minutes.'

He came to the gate but his manner had changed in a way that Milton could not understand. He was aware of the ex-policeman's intense scrutiny; the man was carrying on some sort of conversation but his thoughts were elsewhere. Milton thanked him again.

Tabb, closing the gate behind him, merely raised his hand in acknowledgement.

When he reached the square the bus was already there, a country bus, with one man doubling as driver and conductor. Milton was the only passenger and as the man took his fare he glanced at the sky. 'I think this is likely to be our last trip for today, mister.'

Milton got off at the terminus in the coach station. The great cavernous hall was almost empty and sounds were magnified. Way up in the roof tiny lights struggled against the gloom. Instead of catching another bus he walked out of the station into the forecourt. The kiosk was boarded up. He turned up the slope to the main road, then struck off through a maze of roads which took him through one of the city's industrial areas. The wind had dropped but he felt the cold seeping into his body and quickened his pace.

He came out at last at the junction with Atherton Road below the school. Boys and girls who had been home to lunch were returning for the afternoon session, larking about with snowballs. The same thing would be happening at Mercers' and the duty staff would be vigilant at the school entrances, trying to make sure that the horse-play stopped there. He could think of it with complete detachment. Although he had been away from school for only three days it seemed to belong to another life.

He turned down Bewdley Street. On his left the houses were still occupied, though no one bothered any longer to keep up appearances. Moss grew over the bricks, paintwork was flaking and the little gardens were bursting with weeds. On his right the process had gone a stage further; the houses were empty, for the most part windowless or boarded up. He found number sixteen. The paint was still recognisably lime-

122

green, though the brass knob and the letter-box had gone.

'You've really distinguished yourself, today, Symons, my lad. "A nutter"—that's what you called him, wasn't it? But he was still too smart for you.'

The young detective looked aggrieved. 'There's nothing you can do, sarge, if the chap you're tailing takes a taxi and you're left with only your two feet.' He added after a moment, 'I got the number of the taxi.'

'So?' Hammond blew out a cloud of smoke.

'I picked up the driver later and he said he'd taken Milton out to Laker.'

'Laker? What's he want in that God-forsaken hole?'

'I couldn't say, sarge; the taxi man dropped him in the square and came straight back.'

Hammond thumbed the bristles on his chin. 'Laker— Sergeant Tabb went out that way when he packed up the force. I wonder? First he tries Welsh, and when he finds that Welsh has passed on he has a go at Tabby....'

'Tabb, sarge? I've never heard of him.'

Hammond reached for the phone book. 'You wouldn't have, lad; you still had rubber pants on. Tabby worked here in this nick, but he came to see the light and chucked up police work for farming. I suppose it's better than drink.'

He flicked over the pages of the directory. 'Here we are, "Keston", Dunham Lane, Laker.'

He dialled a number and waited.

'Tabby? ... Hammond ... Doug Hammond from Central....' After a lengthy conversation they got to business. 'Chap calling himself Stuart—Charles Stuart, would you believe?—real name, Milton, a schoolmaster ... No, he hasn't necessarily done anything but he's behaving in a bloody odd way. Anyway, he took a taxi out to Laker this morning, then disappeared into the wide blue yonder. Ringing you is a long shot ... You've seen him? ... Good! What did he want? ... Crime fiction? Was he asking questions about any particular case or about crime in general? ... Just general ... Well, thanks, old man. It takes all sorts. I'll buy you a jar next time you're this way ... Not bloody likely, not in this weather ... Anyway, thanks again.'

Hammond dropped the receiver and swivelled round to face Symons.

'Apparently he went to Laker to see Tabby; said he wrote detective stories and wanted background. He wasn't interested in any particular case, just police methods in general. God help him! As though we had any.'

'It could be the truth, sarge. He tried Welsh and when there was no joy there he goes to see the sergeant.'

Hammond lit one cigarette from the butt of another. 'If I thought he was stringing me on I'd do him for wasting police time. Anyway, the brass don't approve of our spending any more time on him so pack it in.'

'Suits me, sarge.'

Hammond glanced at the clock. 'Ten past two and I haven't had any lunch yet.'

He stooped to light his gas fire but after a brief flicker of flame it went out; the meter needed a coin. He searched through his change but he had no tenpenny pieces, so he kept his coat on and sat in front of the unlit fire. Snow was piled on the window-sill and even on the ledges of the individual panes, it reflected and seemed to intensify the grey light, giving the room a false brightness. After a little while he got up and fetched his notebook from the wardrobe. He opened it on his knees and turned over the first page without looking at what he had written. At the top of the second page he put the date: Thursday 11th November.

He felt the need to write down what had happened and the memories he had recalled, but the words would not come, only pictures. The pictures were extraordinarily vivid and detailed. The lime-green door with its brass knob which shone in the sunshine and felt warm to his hand; Tabb looking at him with an expression that he could not fathom; Christine on the bed in that cramped little room. . . .

There was something missing, something which he could not recall, a link between those things which fitted and those which did not.

Over the bed there had been a framed photograph of a newly married couple, presumably Christine's parents. The girl wore a bridal veil over curly fair hair which was cut short. The man was tall and slim with a fair moustache and he looked tentative, unsure of himself.

He could see the blue cane chair with articles of clothing draped over it. Christine's dress, which had stripes of white, orange and brown; her panties and her brassière, which trailed on the floor. On the dressing-table there was a watch, a wrist-watch. . . .

The picture faded as abruptly as it had come and he could not recall it.

'Of what are you afraid?'

'Of guilt.'

'Of what are you guilty?'

'Of murder.'

He turned to his notebook and after sitting for a long time with his pen poised, he wrote, 'Tabb suspects'.

He did not hear footsteps on the stairs and when the door opened after a perfunctory knock he was startled.

It was Julie. She stood there looking at him in astonishment.

'What on earth. . . ?' She came over to him. 'Are you trying to economise or something?'

'No, I didn't have any tenpenny pieces.' He was trying hard to bring himself back to the present, to sound normal. 'What are you doing home?'

'You know I'm off from two till half past three. I'm on my way back now. Hold on a minute.'

She was gone but back again a moment later with her handbag.

'Here, let me get there.'

She put two coins in the meter and took his matches to light the fire.

'Mother's just told me you were up here.'

'I'll pay you. . . .'

'Don't worry, I'll see you do. I'm off again at six so I'll look in then.' She looked at him with anxiety. 'What's the matter with you? You look like death warmed up.'

'Nothing, I'm all right. If you're off at six, I don't suppose. . . .'

'You don't suppose what?'

'That you'd go out with me again?'

125

'Why not? I must dash now. See you.' The door slammed and he heard her running down the stairs; the front door opened and shut and she was gone. She had left behind that faint odour which tantalised him, part perfume, part something else.

He continued to sit in his overcoat until he was uncomfortably hot, then he took it off and put it in the wardrobe. When he was back in his chair he picked up his notebook once more and added: 'I can't believe that....'

He was interrupted by someone ringing the front door bell, then he heard a murmur of voices and footsteps on the stairs. There was a timid knock at the door, which he did not answer at once, for he had grown used to people knocking then walking in.

'Come in.'

The door opened, it was Elizabeth.

She had come straight from school and she carried her briefcase stuffed with books. She was wearing a grey dufflecoat of which he had often expressed disapproval and her face was rosy with cold. She stood by the door, looking at him shyly. He did not know what to say.

'Mummy thought you didn't want to see her but she wondered ... that is to say, I wondered if you would talk to me?'

He took her coat and put her to sit in the only chair while he sat, awkwardly, on the bed. He saw her looking round, taking everything in, and becoming increasingly bewildered. Her normally smooth brow was wrinkled in a little frown. He found himself looking at her as a stranger and for the first time he realised how like her mother she was.

'I can't explain.' He said it defensively, and accompanied the words with a gesture which seemed to take in much more than the drab little room.

She took a little bundle of letters from her briefcase and handed them to him.

'When mummy knew that you weren't at the house she thought we'd better go there and collect the post. There was post for us too—for her and for me. You don't mind?'

'Why should I mind? I told your mother that you can both go back to the house whenever you want to.'

126

She wore a dark-blue woollen frock which fitted her figure. His eyes followed the firm line of her breasts, her neck and chin, the delicacy of her lips and the large, solemn eyes with their fine, arching brows and dark lashes.

'Mr Bates is very anxious to see you, daddy. Apparently he's been ringing the house and he couldn't understand why there was never any answer.'

'How did you find out that I was here?'

'I think somebody in the police told mummy.'

There was no contact, nothing he could say to her now any more than when they lived under the same roof. If he had managed to speak to her that night at the bus-stop, what could he have said?

'Mother's had a terrible time, you know.'

'Mother'—she was trying to sound objective; it was almost as though she had said, 'your wife'.

He realised now that the barrier between them had not been Jean's obscene innuendo but Christine, the girl on the bed.

There were more footsteps on the stairs, followed by a knock on his door. This time it was the landlady with a tray of tea.

'I thought, seeing you had a visitor, you might like some tea.'

She was wearing a tight black skirt and one of her see-through blouses. He watched Elizabeth sizing her up, or trying to.

He thanked the landlady for the tea but made no introductions. She held her ground for a moment or two then gave way gracefully.

'Well, I'll leave you to it, I expect you want to talk.'

A fresh thought occurred to him. 'Who did you ask for when you came in?'

She flushed. 'The policeman said that you were calling yourself Stuart.'

Was she ashamed for him?

'Would you like some tea?'

'I'll do it.' She busied herself with the tea-things, glad of the distraction.

'Daddy, is it impossible to go back to where we were?'

She was standing close to him, offering him his tea and he

127

was very conscious of her nearness; even, it seemed to him, the warmth of her body. He felt as a spirit must feel when reduced to table rapping as the only means of communication.

'Is that what your mother wants?'

'It's what I want. I'm sure it's what she wants too.' She sipped her tea to keep herself in countenance. 'Even if nothing had happened to Ken. . . .'

He could not allow her to go on.

'I'm sorry, Elizabeth.'

'But you won't do anything?' There were tears in her voice.

'I can't. I tried to explain to your mother but I can't put it into words. I'm not being vindictive, I don't even feel hurt or wronged, but there are things that I must do.'

He glanced round the room as though it symbolised something that he was trying to express. 'This has nothing to do with your mother or with you, it would have happened anyway, sooner or later.'

'I see.'

They were silent for a long time.

'Didn't you ought to be going home? It's gone five and your mother will be worried.'

She looked at him quickly, then she stood up and started to put on her coat. At the door, with her briefcase in her hand, she stopped and looked back.

'It's all right for me to come again?'

'Yes, of course.'

When she was gone he felt both relieved and ashamed.

Julie arrived to find him still sitting in front of the fire.

'Mother said you've had a visitor.'

'My daughter.'

'Oh.'

'Shall we have a meal out?'

'If you like. I've got to change first. Haven't you got anything else to wear?'

'Not here.'

'It doesn't matter. I thought it might cheer you up to put on something different.'

Christine, Elizabeth, Julie. Sometimes they got mixed up in his mind and he could not focus clearly the image of any one of them.

Chapter Nine

ALTHOUGH HAMMOND HAD officially dropped his
investigation of the schoolmaster, Milton was still very much
in his mind. The man was an oddity, with a blend of guile and
naivety which puzzled and intrigued him. His interest was
almost proprietorial and he felt that he had a right to satisfy
his curiosity.

The idea of Milton posing as a writer of crime stories
seemed to Hammond as crack-brained as the rest of his
behaviour. One might walk out of one's house and job,
change one's name and go to live in some back street to
paint pictures or start a brothel, but not, in the sergeant's
opinion, to do anything as futile and innocent as writing
thrillers.

It happened that he had to go to Mercers' that afternoon
in connection with some stolen cigarettes which had been
traced to two boys at the school, and he was in the headmaster's office when the bell went for the end of the afternoon session.

Bates stood at his window, watching the milling mob
flooding out of the main doors and slowly sorting itself out.

'Well, sergeant, thank you for keeping me informed. I must
confess that I am not surprised about the two boys concerned.'

Hammond was being dismissed, but he sat on.

'There is another matter, Mr Bates, and I'd be glad if you
would keep this strictly to yourself.'

Bates returned to his chair, sat down, tucked in his chin
and straightened his blotter.

'I'm interested in a member of your staff.'

'Indeed?' Bates could not quite hide his concern.

'Mr Milton.'

'Ah!' The relief was obvious. Bates had feared something
new. All headmasters are convinced that they are seated on
powder kegs.

'I understand that Mr Milton has leave of absence?'

'Yes, all this business with his wife upset him. He needed a break.'

'He seems to be behaving very oddly.'

Bates spread his hands. 'I'm not surprised. There's been so much gossip about the poor man, and your people haven't helped.'

Hammond wanted him to talk without being questioned, but Bates was too wary.

'I understand that he has been on the staff here for about six years?'

'About that.'

'A comparative newcomer to the district.'

Bates frowned. 'I suppose you could say that though I heard only recently that he did his teaching practice here—not in this school but in the city.'

'Teaching practice?'

'I'm sorry. Trade jargon. When you are doing your post-graduate education year you have to spend ten weeks teaching in a school. It seems that Milton did his ten weeks at Atherton Road School.'

'Really?'

Bates smiled a tolerant smile. 'Apparently he paid them a visit the day before yesterday. Rowse, the headmaster, mentioned it to me on the phone. It seems the poor fellow behaved rather oddly there.'

It was clear that Bates was not putting himself out to improve the Milton image and for some obscure reason Hammond held it against him.

'Until this business with his wife, has Mr Milton's conduct been entirely satisfactory?'

'Entirely.'

Hammond was not sure whether he had got something or not. The fact that Milton had spent ten weeks in the city as a student teacher might be significant, but how? He promised himself that he would call on the Atherton Road head in the morning and find out in what way Milton had conducted himself so oddly.

While he was in the neighbourhood, Hammond decided to visit the flat in Gordon Street where, according to Symons,

130

Milton had visited someone called Sparkes.

A few minutes later he was ringing the bell in the yellow door.

'Mrs Sparkes?'

A plump woman, pleasant looking, with dyed hair. 'I'm Mrs Wilson.'

'I thought the name was Sparkes. . . .'

'That's my sister and her husband, I live with them.'

Hammond showed his warrant card. 'May I come in?'

The flat smelt of savoury cooking, warm and palate tickling. He was taken into the living room and introduced to Mrs Sparkes. She sat in front of the fire, fragile and colourless. A tall, thin youth who had been sitting reading, got up and left the room. The table was partly laid for a meal.

'I hope I'm not delaying your meal?'

'There's no hurry, Mr Sparkes isn't due back for over an hour.' Mrs Wilson's plump features looked like an anxious baby's. 'There's nothing wrong, is there?'

'Nothing in any way affecting you.' Hammond was standing by the window, looking down into the street. He had to play it by ear. 'It's just that we've been getting complaints about a gang of lads causing trouble in the kids' playground across the way. As you're on the top floor I thought you might be in a good position to see what goes on there.'

Mrs Wilson frowned. 'I've never seen anything. What sort of trouble?'

Hammond shrugged. 'You know what some of these teen-aged lads are like, frightening the youngsters and smashing up equipment.'

'No, I've never seen anything of that sort, have you, Joyce?'

The invalid shook her head. 'Never.'

'What about your lad—the boy I saw just now?'

'You don't think that he—?'

'Certainly not, Mrs Wilson, I'm sure he's a well-conducted young man; he certainly looks it. I just wondered whether he might know which group of yobs is causing the trouble.'

'You can ask him but I doubt it; he lives in his books and his school work.'

'Bright, is he? What school does he go to?'

'Mercers'.'

'Good for him.'

'They're putting him in for the Oxford exam.'

'Really? Well, that's something to be proud of.'

'Of course, changing schools hasn't helped, but he's settling down.'

'You haven't been here long, then?'

'Five months. We lived in Bristol but my husband died so Alan and I came down here to live with my sister.'

'So you're newcomers?'

'In a way, but not really. My husband and I both came from the city. We lived in Bewdley Street for twenty years after we were married but he was promoted and moved to Bristol not long before Alan was born.'

For once in his humdrum existence Hammond had the 'Eureka' experience but he was careful not to let it show. Bewdley Street and the name Wilson had clicked in his mind, or he thought they had.

'Bewdley Street? They're pulling it down now, aren't they?'

Mrs Wilson sighed. 'I know, it's getting so that you don't recognise any of the old places.'

Hammond decided to leave. He needed time to think before he pushed his luck any further.

'I must be off. Thanks for putting up with me, and if you see anything going on in that playground perhaps you'll give us a buzz?'

And he hadn't even mentioned the schoolmaster.

Back at the station, Hammond felt less sure of himself but he caught Chief Inspector Moone before the latter left for his semi-detached, his four children, two dogs and harassed wife.

'You're not still on about that damned schoolmaster, Hammond?'

'I could be, sir. Do you remember the Bewdley Street murder? Young girl found strangled in her parents' bedroom?'

'Vaguely. I remember hearing about it but it was before I joined this force.'

'Me too. I was a beat copper up in the smoke then, but I used to hear them talking about it when I first came here. Can you remember the name of the family?'

'Is this double-your-money, or something? I don't know, I've got a feeling it was Wilkins.'

'What about Wilson?'

'Wilson, that's it. If you knew, what did you ask for?'

'Where would the case-file be now, sir?'

'At H.Q. I suppose. They never cracked it so technically the file is still open.'

'Could you have it sent over for me to take a look?'

'I suppose I could if I had a good enough reason.'

In the end, Moone was persuaded.

'But understand this, no action without my say-so. If it ever comes to re-opening we shall have Mr Goddard in on it from square one.'

'Fair enough, sir.'

'All right, I'll see to it in the morning.'

'What's wrong with tonight, sir?'

The evening was clear and frosty and the snow still stood. The papers and the radio were filling space and time with statistics to prove that this was the earliest cold snap on record and the pundits prophesied a long, hard winter. Milton and Julie walked arm-in-arm to the bus-stop in the green and Julie wore a little fur cap which partly covered her ears and made her look, Milton said, like a Russian.

They ate kebabs at a Greek restaurant and drank a carafe of wine which tasted like varnish. Afterwards they went to a cinema and saw a French film which seemed to take place throughout in semi-darkness.

They arrived home just after eleven.

'I'll make some cocoa.'

When she came back she said, 'Have it in my room, it's more comfortable.'

It was the first time he had seen her room. It was bright, she had furnished and decorated it herself, and if the carpet dazzled and the furniture looked plastic, to Milton it had the appeal of something that was uniquely and intimately hers.

'Like it?'

'It's very nice.'

There were two chairs and they sat one on each side of the gas-fire to drink their cocoa. She had on her white jumper

133

and tartan skirt. As he was drinking she caught his eye and grinned, a companionable and confiding grin. He knew nothing of this girl and yet, at times, she held him in the hollow of her hand. In her company he seemed able to gather up his troubles and push them back in their box, slamming the lid shut.

'There's no fool like an old fool.'

'What's that supposed to mean? You're not old.'

He said nothing and she went on: 'The trouble with you is that you're always trying to work out the odds.'

She put her empty mug on the mantelpiece. 'I'm going to get ready for bed.'

He stood up.

'Don't go unless you want to; sit there and enjoy it.'

She took off her jumper and skirt and put them away in the wardrobe, then, with a wrap over her slip, she picked up her sponge bag.

'Shan't be long.'

She was gone about ten minutes and when she came back she was still wearing her wrap, but she threw a little handful of underclothes on the bed and he knew that she was naked underneath the wrap. He could not take his eyes off her.

'Do you fancy me?'

He stammered, 'You know that I find you very attractive.'

'Well, that's a start.'

She came over to him and started to undo his tie, and when he was wearing only his shirt he found the courage to remove her wrap. He told himself that he had never seen anyone so lovely. After Jean's well covered body her slim perfection entranced him.

She grinned up at him. 'Come on!'

And a little later when they were under the bedclothes, 'Relax, let yourself go. You could be in worse places.'

When it happened it came as the most natural thing in the world, yet he had never had an experience like it. For once in his life he ceased bothering his head about consequences and it was as though he had been transported to some other world where he floated among huge iridescent bubbles which grew and burst and grew again; for an instant it seemed that he had only to reach out and he would have

134

within his grasp something inexpressibly beautiful and precious ... The moment passed but he had no regrets. Soon self-consciousness returned.

'Thank you, Julie. I'm sorry it was over so soon.'

'Who timed it? Anyway we'll try again directly.'

'I've never managed it more than once.'

'You will tonight, just stop talking and leave it to me.'

Later on she asked him with a faint chuckle in her voice, 'Is it true that you're a schoolmaster?'

It was the first question she had asked him about himself.

'CHRISTINE JANE WILSON: Murder. Information received: 6.47pm. August 19th 1956.'

The contents of the file were spread out on Hammond's desk. Hundreds of statements clipped together in bundles; envelopes stuffed with photographs; reports from experts; reports from detectives; street and house plans; even duty rosters and cuttings from local newspapers. It was all there and Hammond knew from experience the thousands of man-hours which go into such a case; the boredom, the frustration and, in this instance, the bitter taste of ultimate failure.

'Christine Jane Wilson, born 12th June 1939. Daughter of James John and Jane Catherine Wilson of 16, Bewdley Street.'

This went with a small packet of photographs labelled 'Deceased'.

The first was a studio portrait of a young girl. Fair, wavy, short hair. A broad, intelligent forehead, good features; a pretty girl, a girl any man would look twice at, but there was something about her which sounded a warning note. Hammond was struck by it.

The other photographs showed her naked and dwelt on her injuries.

Statement by James John Wilson, father of the deceased:

' ... At six o'clock on Sunday evening, 19th August, I returned home after spending a week's holiday in Weston-super-Mare. My wife was with me but my daughter, Christine, had decided not to come with us and had remained at home, alone. As she was a most reliable girl we were not worried about leaving her.

'The front door was not locked. I opened it and called out

that we were back but there was no answer. I thought this was strange because she was expecting us and, in any case, she would not have gone out leaving the door unlocked.

'In the kitchen we found the table laid with a meal for two —cold ham and tongue and bread already cut. My wife remarked that Christine had got a meal for us, but when we came to look more closely we saw that the food had been there for some time, the meat and the bread had dried up.

'We began to be worried and I decided to look upstairs before doing anything else. I went to Christine's room in case she was lying down, but her room was empty and everything looked as usual. I then went to the main bedroom where my wife and I sleep and there I found Christine on the bed. I saw at once that she was dead...'

Note on deceased submitted by Mr G. A. Rowse M.A., headmaster Atherton Road Grammar School:

'Christine Wilson was a pupil in the sixth form of this school, which she attended from the age of eleven. Christine was an able, hard working girl. She obtained nine passes with good grades in the Ordinary Level examinations of the General Certificate of Education and she was studying History, French and English in the sixth. I expected her to do well in the Advanced Level examinations and to obtain a place at university.

'At no time during her six years with us did she ever give cause for concern about her work or her conduct. She was popular with pupils and staff.

'In a mixed school there is necessarily a certain freedom of association between boys and girls, they work together and often share recreational activities, but I have never seen the slightest evidence to suggest that Christine had an over-developed interest in the opposite sex. My staff and I are of the opinion that she had rather less interest in boys than the average girl of her age....'

Hammond continued to turn over the material. To some extent it was a lucky dip; he could not possibly read it all.

Statement by Rosemary Todd:

'I am a pupil in the sixth form of Atherton Road Grammar School and I was a friend of the deceased. About six months ago Christine told me that she had a man-friend. I asked

136

her if she didn't mean a boy-friend and she replied that she meant what she said and that she didn't go out with boys. I asked her who the man was and she said I would be very surprised if I knew. Another time I asked her if she had sex with this man and she said that she did. I said that I thought she was being very silly and taking an awful risk but she laughed and said she didn't think she could have a baby if she tried.

'Sometime later, it must have been the end of April because it was early in the summer term, she said she wanted to have Sunday away from home and that she had told her parents she was spending the day with me. She asked me to back her up if there were any questions asked. I said I would but I didn't like it very much. This happened on two or three other Sundays in the summer term. I asked her if she spent these Sundays with her man-friend and she said that she did. She also told me that she had a second man-friend who she went with. I did not believe her and I said so but she said that it took more than one man to satisfy her. I thought she was making it up.

'I have thought over very carefully everything I can remember that she said to me but I can think of nothing that might help to identify the man or men she was talking about....'

Next came the report of the pathologist.

After describing the condition of the body and saying that death was due to manual strangulation, he went on to state his conclusions concerning the time of death: 'In my opinion death occurred within two hours either side of mid-day on Saturday 18th August. It is difficult to be more precise, but my preference would be for the later rather than the earlier time.'

Later in his report he described at length his further investigations in so far as they might help to establish the identity of the girl's assailant:

'As stated above, the blood-group of the deceased was found to be A. She was a non-secretor, which means that group specific substances were not present in body fluids other than the blood. The fact that contaminated seminal fluid removed from the vagina gave a clear group B reaction means, therefore, that the man with whom she had sexual intercourse immediately prior to her death must belong to that group.'

It was past midnight and Hammond's original enthusiasm had evaporated. He was beginning to think that the threads linking the schoolmaster with this twenty year old crime were more slender than he had believed. To boost his ego he summarised them:

1. Christine Wilson was murdered on August 18th 1956.
2. Milton was a student teacher at Atherton Road for ten weeks in the spring term of that year.
3. Milton was studying newspaper files for the second half of 1956.
4. Milton taught history, which was one of Christine Wilson's sixth form subjects.
5. Christine told another girl that she had a man-friend and that the girl would be very surprised if she knew who he was.
6. Milton had visited Mrs Wilson, the dead girl's mother.
7. Milton had visited Sergeant Tabb and tried to visit Inspector Welsh. Both these men had been involved in the police investigation of Christine's death.

He read through what he had written and thought it looked rather better than he had expected. He turned again to the contents of the file.

Dozens of negative statements from neighbours and friends. Then two which seemed to offer more promise but had got them nowhere:

Statement by Joyce Pollard of 13, Bewdley Street:

'I live in the house opposite the Wilsons. On the night of Friday 17th August it was very hot and I could not sleep. Our bedroom window was wide open and I could hear the slightest noise from the street. I cannot say what time it was but it was just beginning to get light. I heard footsteps on the pavement opposite, then whoever it was went up the steps to one of the houses. I cannot say for certain that it was the Wilsons' house. I heard a door open, there was a whispered conversation and I thought it was a man and a woman talking but I could not be sure. After that the door closed and I did not hear any more. I did not get out of bed because I did not want to disturb my husband.'

It looked very much as though the killer had arrived at number sixteen in the early hours of Saturday morning.

Statement by Nora Smith of 27, Bewdley Street:

'I run the general store on the corner of Bewdley Street and on Saturday morning, 18th August, I was in my shop as usual. At about ten o'clock Christine Wilson came in and bought two ounces of cooked ham and two ounces of tongue. She also bought half-a-pound of butter and a loaf of bread.

'Christine seemed just as usual except that she hadn't bothered to dress up. Her hair was untidy and I had the impression that she had just got out of bed. I remarked that it wouldn't be long before her mum and dad were home and she laughed and said she'd got another day of freedom. She was always a pleasant friendly girl.'

Presumably, apart from the murderer, the shopkeeper was the last person to see Christine alive.

It was a little after one in the morning when Hammond left the police station to go home to his bungalow, his dog, his two daughters and his patient wife.

Chapter Ten

MILTON GOT OUT of bed with infinite caution to avoid waking Julie. After sleeping like a baby for four or five hours he had lain awake for a while staring at the ceiling, trying to order his thoughts. He collected his clothes, went to the bathroom, then to his own room to dress. He felt unnaturally calm. He knew that he ought to be experiencing some strong emotion: elation, shame, self-satisfaction, self-disgust; but he felt nothing, nothing except a vague gratitude and tenderness to the girl in the bed. He had known the same serenity when he had been given an injection of pentathol before his appendix operation.

He went downstairs to breakfast at the usual time. There were four or five other lodgers breakfasting with him but he took no notice of them. He was aware of the landlady watching him as he ate his bacon and egg and he thought that she knew or had guessed what had happened. He reflected how surprising it was that this should not trouble him. After breakfast he went back to his room, where he had left the gas fire burning.

He noticed that the snow on the window ledges had gone and it was raining.

As he sat in front of the fire his serenity gave place to depression.

'It is a law of neurotic diseases that these obsessive acts serve the impulse more and more and come nearer and nearer to the original forbidden act.' He had read that in one of his books.

Hammond had obtained grudging permission from Chief Inspector Moone to talk to Rowse, the headmaster of Atherton Road School, and he had stretched his brief to include the head of the history department, who had also been there in Milton's time as a student teacher. He told

140

them in confidence that he was making enquiries about Milton but did not mention the girl.

Rowse was a large, heavy man, slow of speech but mentally wide awake. He was bald except for a fringe at the back, and when faced with an awkward question he would pass his hand over his shining cranium time and time again until he had thought what to say. The history man, Pride, was small and wiry with a mass of white hair and a sly sense of humour.

'Yes, I remember Milton when he was a student-teacher here. He was a good lad—keen, but weren't we all at that age? I haven't come across him since although we teach the same subject in the same town. He doesn't attend the history seminars, probably because his headmaster is less persuasive than ours.'

Rowse sat back in his chair, making it creak under the strain. 'I've seen him once or twice at inter-schools meetings and we've exchanged the odd word. I remember him vaguely when he was here as a student teacher but we neither of us mentioned that. He strikes me as a prickly sort of chap. The odd thing is, he looked in here earlier this week. God knows why. He pushed off as soon as he saw me.'

'I know it's asking a lot,' Hammond said, 'but can you tell me if he taught or came into contact with Christine Wilson when he was here?'

He saw the sharp, surprised glances exchanged by the two men.

'The girl who was murdered? Are you still on about that? I thought it was the business about Milton's wife.'

'Never let up, sir, that's our motto.'

Rowse shook his head. 'I don't know about Pride but I couldn't tell you anything one way or another. Student teachers come and go and they don't usually make much impact on the place.'

Pride frowned. 'I might be able to find something. I record the more momentous daily happenings in the history department in little black books. Something to read in the long lazy days of my retirement. If you'll excuse me....' He stopped at the door. 'When was it? 56? 57?'

'56.'

He was gone two or three minutes and returned with a thin octavo notebook.

'Let's see. The students come in the spring term ... here we are, Arthur Milton ... Actually he was here for twelve weeks, not the usual ten. The university term ends a fortnight before ours and the student teachers are only required to work the ten-week term.'

'But he stayed on?'

'Gave up a fortnight of his vacation. It happens with some of the keen ones.'

'Often?'

'Occasionally. ...'

'Here's his timetable ... He taught seventeen periods a week, four with my sixth form group which included Christine Wilson.'

'You never thought to mention that while the enquiry was on?'

'It never occurred to me. Why should it? Milton finished here in the last week of March; Christine was killed sometime during the following August. We had no reason to connect him with her.'

Rowse had been quiet for some time, now he interrupted. 'You can't really think that Milton killed that poor girl, sergeant?'

'Oh, I don't think anything, sir. I just ask questions.'

Pride was still turning the pages of his notebook. 'He took his history sixth to the records department of the museum one Saturday afternoon, there's dedication for you!'

'Would Christine have been one of that party?'

'I've no idea but I expect she was. She would go along with her mates. In any case, all the girls fancied Milton, come to think of it.'

'Fancied him?'

'Well, he was a good looking youngster and he had that lost-dog look which gets 'em where they keep their maternal instinct.'

'Nothing more you can tell me?' Hammond was unreasonably disappointed.

'What else is there to tell?' Pride shrugged his thin shoulders. 'As far as I'm concerned he was a very good student teacher and that's all there was to it.'

Milton had his notebook open on his knees and he had written on a fresh page: 'Friday November 12th. I had no right. Such a terrible risk.'

At eleven o'clock the landlady came up to make his bed and he decided to go out.

'It's raining, you know and the snow has almost gone already.'

He took his mackintosh and walked to Commercial Road, but instead of making for the green he turned up Bewdley Street. He walked, as always, with the same slow strides, seemingly oblivious of the rain. Outside number sixteen he stopped and stood looking up at the windows, which were roughly boarded over. He had no hat and no umbrella and the rain was dripping from his hair and running down his neck. After standing there for some minutes he walked up to the front door and tried to push it open, but it did not yield. He pushed harder, then lunged against it with his shoulder. It gave a little. He tried hammering at it with the sole of his shoe, aiming blow after blow. The door had been nailed shut from the inside and the nails were giving reluctantly under his sustained attack but he was drawing attention from the other side of the street.

It seemed to him that the door was a last barrier between him and the truth which he had set out to discover, and in the end it gave, swinging slowly open on its rusty hinges. Almost exhausted, he went inside.

There were gaps in the flooring and fungoid growths protruded between the planks of the wainscot. But the stairs were still in place, though the banisters had gone and two of the treads were missing. To his surprise he found evidence that somebody had been sleeping in the kitchen. There were two filthy blankets on the floor, a number of tins and bottles, and the stench was appalling. He noticed that the back door was not secured in any way, so it would have been possible for him to have camped out here as this nameless tramp had done. He wondered if he would have done so had the idea occurred to him.

The thought intrigued and momentarily diverted him. He

143

had exchanged his comfortable house in Barnfield Close for a cheap lodging-house in Canal Street and he knew that his reasons for doing so were more complex than he had admitted to himself. In addition to all the rest there was the attraction of letting oneself go, of not bothering to do this or that, of establishing an equilibrium at a lower level, perhaps at the base-level represented by this tramp's squalid pitch.

He turned away and went up the stairs, keeping close to the wall. On the landing the doors of both bedrooms stood a little open, but not enough for him to see inside. The main bedroom was on his right and it required an effort of will to push the door wide. In that instant he would not have been surprised to see the room as he had seen it twenty years before.

The room was empty. Much of the ceiling had collapsed into little heaps of plaster on the floor, but the wall-paper was the same: vertical strings of red roses, damp and faded but still recognisable. There was a pale patch where the bed-head had been and another where the dressing-table had stood. Even the wedding photograph over the bed had left its rectangular imprint behind. If anybody had occupied the house since the Wilsons it could not have been for long.

Milton did not go into the room, but he stood in the door-way for a very long time. Now and then his lips moved and occasionally he murmured a word or a phrase.

The silence was complete yet, suddenly, for no apparent reason, he turned as though startled and stared at the door of the other room. It was open a few inches as it had been when he came up the stairs. Nothing had changed, yet he continued to stare as though at some astonishing phenomenon.

He could not have said how long he stood there, the water dripping from his mackintosh on to the floor. A car drove down the street and pulled up not far away; then, at last, he turned from the room and went slowly down the stairs. He felt tired, more tired than he had ever been in his life before, and as he walked down Bewdley Street he dragged his feet like an old man. He had one more task to perform, then he would be able to rest.

He turned up towards the green, crossed the bridge over the canal and passed the café without a glance. At the junction he waited, mechanically, for the traffic; then he crossed and waited at the bus-stop, making no attempt to get shelter from the steady downpour. A bus came and he took a ticket for the city centre.

The Central Police Station, next to the library, is red brick with Waterhouse turrets and towers. Milton went up the granite steps, pushed through the swing doors and found himself in a small room with a counter which had been carved out of the original entrance hall. A young constable at the counter looked at him with curiosity.

'I want to see Sergeant Hammond.'

'What's your name, sir?'

'Milton—Arthur Milton.'

'And your business?'

'Just tell him I'm here.'

The constable went to a telephone at the back and carried on a conversation in low tones. Hardly had he dropped the receiver than Hammond came through a door behind the counter.

'Well, here's a surprise! I was thinking of coming to see you.' Hammond looked him up and down. 'You're soaked!'

'It doesn't matter, is there somewhere we can talk?'

He followed Hammond through a maze of corridors into a small office which had two desks, a filing cabinet and no window.

'Sit down. What's it all about, then?'

Hammond's manner was friendly, patronising. How to deal with nervous children and lunatics.

'I've just come from Bewdley Street.'

'Bewdley Street? They're knocking it down, aren't they?'

'I killed Christine Wilson.'

'Christine Wilson?'

'The Bewdley Street murder.'

'That was a long time ago.'

'Twenty years.'

'You've been a long time getting round to telling us about it.'

Milton made a gesture of helplessness. 'I can't explain, I

145

don't understand myself, but I've lived all these years without really knowing.'

'And now you do know?'

'I've been over the ground, I've checked all the facts, I've forced myself to face the truth.'

'You went to see Sergeant Tabb.'

'He told you? I thought he would. I found out that he had worked on the case.'

'He said that you talked to him about police methods in general, not about any particular case.'

Milton was puzzled. 'I don't understand why he said that. I told him that I wanted information about the Christine Wilson case for a book I was going to write. He was very cautious; in the end I thought that he suspected me.'

Hammond looked at him for some time in silence. In the end he said, 'This is going to take us a long time, so I'll tell you what I'm going to do. I'm going to send you back to your digs to get out of those wet clothes. Then you can come back here and we'll find out what it's all about.'

He was too tired to argue. A Panda car took him to Canal Street. The landlady was out and the constable stayed with him while he dried himself and changed into a sports jacket and slacks. When he returned to the police station he was not taken to Hammond's office but to a larger office on the first floor, where a plump, jovial-looking man sat at a desk with Hammond beside him. A woman constable was placed near the door, a notebook on her lap.

'This is Detective Chief Inspector Moone, Mr Milton.'

'Before we go any further, Mr Milton,' Moone said, 'I must warn you that you do not have to say anything but anything you do say may be taken down in writing and used in evidence. Do you understand that warning?'

Milton nodded with impatience. 'Of course! I shouldn't have come here if—'

Moone interrupted. 'Good! This interview begins at 13.07 hours. It is not uncommon for someone to confess to a crime which he did not commit and so waste a lot of police time.'

'I assure you—'

'So it would help us a great deal if you would consent to a blood test.'

'A blood test?'

Moone nodded. 'We know the blood group of the man who killed Christine. If you are of the same group it will not prove that you killed her, but if you are of a different group it will be evidence that you did not.'

'But I've told Sergeant Hammond—'

'Are you willing to have a sample of blood taken for testing, Mr Milton?'

'Well, yes. . . .'

'Good! I've arranged for someone from the pathology department of the hospital to be here shortly. The sample will be taken back to their laboratory and tested. Then we shall have a better idea of where we stand.'

It was not going as he had supposed that it would. It was almost as though the large, placid man behind the desk was determined to disregard anything he had to say.

Moone removed the contents of a fat pocket file and started to turn over the documents it contained.

'Whether or not you killed Christine Wilson, it seems that you may be in a position to provide new evidence which will explain some of the circumstances in which she died. So, if you agree, we shall ask you some questions about your relationship with her.'

'It was Saturday, 18th August 1956. I—'

'That was the day she was killed, Mr Milton; we need to start a good deal further back. When, and in what circumstances, did you first meet her?'

The office was in the front of the building and the noise of the traffic was continuous. The windows were grimy and that, with the unrelenting rain, made it impossible to see more than the vague outline of buildings across the street.

He told them how he had been sent to Atherton Road for his teaching practice, how he had been allocated certain periods with the history sixth, how he had taken his pupils to the museum to see old records. . . .

'So you asked her to have tea with you?'

'Yes.'

'Why her rather than any of the others?'

He had to stop and think; he had never asked himself that question.

'Was it because she was a very pretty girl?'

'No, I don't think so. She stayed behind when the others had gone. In fact, she usually did.' He smiled. 'Christine always had some question she wanted to ask....'

'In other words she made a dead set at you?'

He was shocked. 'No, it wasn't like that at all.'

'Anyway, after having tea with her you took her to the pictures. What happened then?'

'Nothing happened. I walked home with her—as far as the end of her street.'

'And on Monday morning it was back to normal—teacher and pupil, is that right?'

'Well, not quite. We met in the evenings once or twice and we went for walks after school. One Saturday we went by bus to Rudyard and spent most of the day walking by the lake.'

'During this time, did you make love?'

'No, nothing like that.'

'Did you kiss her?'

'Yes, sometimes.'

Were they laughing at him?

So far Hammond had said nothing, now he asked a question: 'You did an extra two weeks at Atherton Road, after the university term was over, why did you do that?'

'I should have done that in any case. I wanted to get in as much teaching as possible.'

'Then you went home to Bristol for your Easter vacation. Did you hear from Christine during that time?'

'No.'

'Did you think about her?'

'Yes.'

'In what way?'

He was trying to be honest but it was difficult. 'Affectionately, but I realised that I had come very near to making a fool of myself, perhaps ruining my career.'

'In other words you were a bit relieved to be out of it?'

'I suppose so.'

There seemed to be a conspiracy to minimise what he had done, to whitewash him and, far from relaxing his inner tension, it made him feel worse.

The telephone rang and Moone answered it.

148

'Moone here ... Yes, right away....'

He turned to Milton. 'They've come to take the sample.' He glanced up at the clock over the mantelpiece. 'It's two o'clock. Have you had any lunch, Mr Milton?'

'No, but—'

'Neither have we. I suggest that you let them have their sample, then Sergeant Hammond will arrange for you to have a meal. After that we can go on from where we left off.' He glanced across at the woman constable. 'This interview ends at 14.04 hours.'

A break for lunch! It was incredible.

The rain had stopped and the clouds must have thinned, for the buildings opposite were now clearly visible in a misty, golden light. Perhaps the sun was breaking through. There was a row of windows which he had never noticed from ground level, windows with stone pilasters and dummy balconies.

'So it was not until her second visit to your lodgings that you made love?'

Milton nodded. 'That's right.'

'Was she a virgin?'

His reply was barely audible. 'No.'

He was afraid of the next question but he need not have worried.

'And she made two more Sunday visits to you during that term?'

'Yes.'

'Did you ask her to marry you?'

He hesitated; he had never actually proposed to her. 'It was assumed that we would eventually marry; it was a question of waiting until I was settled in a job.'

'But she didn't tell her parents about you; was that your idea or hers?'

'I suggested that we should be properly engaged; people still got engaged in those days.'

'What did she say?'

'That it was our secret and she wanted to keep it that way. She told me not to write to her during the summer vacation, that she would write to me.'

'And did she?'

With a shy movement Milton brought out the grey envelope which he had carefully transferred when he changed his jacket. He took out the photograph and the five letters and spread them on the desk while Moone and Hammond watched him.

Evidence that would have meant so much to the detectives who had spent months investigating the crime. Milton picked out one of the letters and passed it to Moone:

Dearest—,
   I have fixed it so that I shall be here alone in the house all the week while mum and dad are in Weston....

Moone read the letter through carefully, then passed it to Hammond.

'The letter is dated August 10th, the day her parents went on holiday and she asks you to tell her when you will come. What did you do?'

'I had a job, a vacation job, and I couldn't get away.'

'Did you write to tell her?'

'Yes.'

'And you went the following Saturday; did you tell her to expect you then?'

'No, I was going to surprise her.'

The clock over the mantelpiece showed five minutes past four. They had been late starting the afternoon session and Milton had been kept hanging about in an interview room for a long time after he had eaten.

Moone saw his glance at the clock and misinterpreted it. 'The result of your blood test should be here soon. I don't know what takes them so long.'

There were lights in the windows across the road and he could see clearly into one office, where a man was speaking into a microphone, presumably attached to a dictating machine. As he dictated the man swivelled to and fro in his chair.

'You have told us that Christine demanded violence in sex. When did you first have evidence of this?'

'The first time we made love—that Sunday afternoon in my lodgings.'

150

'Did it worry you?'

'Of course.'

'Why?'

Milton did not answer.

'Did it disgust you?'

'No.'

'What then?'

'I could not trust myself.'

'You mean that you were afraid you would not be able to keep yourself in check?'

'Yes.' He added after a moment, in a voice scarcely above a whisper, 'And I was right.'

'Now, tell us about the Saturday when you visited Christine in Bewdley Street.'

He took time to collect his thoughts.

'It was a really hot day; the city was like a huge oven. I arrived at the coach station just after mid-day....'

It was getting dark and Hammond got up to switch on the lights—a trio of bulbs with frilly, glass shades suspended from the ceiling on a long chain.

'Did you ring the door bell?'

'There was no bell, only a knocker.'

'All right, did you knock?'

'I think so, I must have done. I mean, I wouldn't have walked straight in.'

'But there was no answer?'

'No answer. I remember looking up and down the street to see if anybody was watching me, but the whole place seemed to be deserted. I turned the knob, the door opened and I went in.'

'What then?'

'I think I called out ... Yes, I did, I called out, "Christine!" and then I added something like, "It's me, Arthur".'

'Go on.'

He was very pale and little beads of sweat stood out on his forehead. Moone looked at him with concern.

'Are you well enough to go on with this?'

He made a vigorous gesture of impatience. 'For God's sake! ...

'I heard a noise upstairs and I called out again but there

151

was no answer. I looked in the kitchen and the sitting room but they were both empty. Then I went upstairs. . . .'

He broke off and they could see that he was making an effort to reconstruct and put into words the experience which had haunted him ever since. Suddenly he shrugged and seemed to slump in his chair.

'I can't.'

'You can't tell us or you can't remember?'

'I can't remember what happened after I reached the top of the stairs. The next thing I do remember I was standing there on the landing once more, looking into the bedroom, and it was all over. Christine was dead.'

Moone shuffled through a series of photographs which he shielded from Milton's view.

'You have a clear recollection of what you saw, looking into that room?'

'Very clear, almost photographic.'

'Tell me what you saw.'

The telephone rang.

Moone answered it with a movement of impatience. 'Yes?' He reached for a pencil and made one or two notes. 'You will let me have your written report? . . . Thank you.' He replaced the receiver and turned to Milton.

'That was the haematologist. Your blood group is not the same as that of the killer.' He glanced at the file. 'The murderer's group was B, yours is O.'

'But there must be a mistake!'

'There is no mistake about the blood groups, Mr Milton, get that into your head once and for all. If, as the pathologist claimed at the time, the man who killed her was the man who was having intercourse with her, then you are not that man.'

Milton made a small, helpless gesture with his hands.

'I'm guilty. This is absurd! I killed her.'

Moone was looking at him in calm appraisal, doing his best to understand.

'Do you remember killing her?'

'No.'

'Do you remember having intercourse with her on that occasion?'

There was a brief pause but in the end he shook his head and said, 'No.'

'All you remember is being on the landing and seeing her lying there.'

It was a strange experience for the two policemen, having a man maintain his guilt with the same earnestness and in the same pleading tones as so many protest their innocence.

'I tell you, I killed her!'

Moone glanced at the clock. 'This interview ends at 16.35 hours.'

'What does that mean?'

'It means that you are free to go, Mr Milton, but, because you are offering new evidence in this case we shall almost certainly want to talk to you again.'

'I would rather stay here and answer whatever questions you want to ask.'

Moone sighed. 'Very well, but I must have a word with my chief. If you go with Sergeant Hammond he will see that you are looked after until we are ready.'

They provided him with tea, bread-and-butter and a cake, then he was left alone in an interview room for the better part of an hour.

At a little after six Hammond came to fetch him and this time he was taken, again, to Hammond's office.

'Sit down, Mr Milton and try to relax. You should feel relieved—'

'Please let us get on with it.'

Hammond looked at him and shook his head. He had on the desk in front of him the same file which the chief inspector had consulted. He searched in it and came out with a photograph.

'I have here, Mr Milton, several photographs of the room as it was when the police were called in. As far as we know nobody went into the room from the time you left it on the Saturday until the return of the girl's father on Sunday evening. According to his statement, he removed nothing, so it should appear in these photographs just as you saw it.'

'If you'll let me see them. . . .'

'No, I would prefer you to tell me what you remember.'

153

Milton had no difficulty in describing the room as he had seen it.

'The bed, a double bed, was opposite the door; when the door was open there was scarcely any room between it and the foot of the bed. The bed had a lot of brasswork and what wasn't brass was shiny black enamel ... Over the bed there was a framed photograph of a newly married couple—the girl still wore her wedding dress. The window was to the left of the bed and on the other side there was a dressing-table with a swing mirror and a cane chair which had been painted blue and sprayed with gold round the edges. The blue eiderdown and most of the bedclothes were in a heap on the foot of the bed. Do you want me to tell you about. . . ?'

Hammond shook his head. 'Just stick to the room and the furniture for the moment. You say the window was to the left of the bed, but was there anything else on that wall?'

'No, I don't think so, just the window.'

'Did the window have curtains or a blind or what?'

Milton looked puzzled. 'I'm not sure, I suppose it had curtains but I can't remember for certain.'

Hammond shrugged. 'All right, go on. Any more details?'

'Christine's clothes were lying on the cane chair, her striped dress, her panties—oh, yes, her brassière was trailing down from the arm of the chair to the floor.'

'Go on.'

'There were things on the dressing-table—trinkets. I can remember a blue china dish or tray with a watch on it—'

'A watch? What sort of watch?'

'A wrist watch.'

'Christine's?'

'No, it wasn't hers. It had a broad leather strap more like the one I'm wearing now, a man's watch.'

'Could it have been yours?'

'No, I didn't have a watch in those days.'

Hammond passed over one of his photographs. It showed the room as seen from the landing; the door opened to the left and appeared to be touching the foot of the bed, so that nothing could be seen of the left hand side of the room. Everything was as he had described it and the effect on him was profound. The picture over the bed, the dressing table, the cane chair with Christine's clothes, Christine's body....

'You did pretty well, don't you think?'

Milton said nothing.

'Can you see a watch in the china dish on the dressing-table?'

He looked more closely. 'No, the dish is empty.'

Hammond nodded. He was shuffling through the pile of papers on his desk and in the end he handed Milton some typescript clipped together.

'Look at page 3. It's part of an inventory which was made of everything in that room.' Hammond indicated one section with his forefinger. 'Read the bit headed; Top of Dressing-table.'

Milton read the items aloud.

'One swing-mirror in wooden frame on wooden stand.

'One jar of Pond's face-cream.

'One small box of face-powder.

'One china dish in blue and white and gold....'

'No watch?'

'No, but there was a watch.'

Hammond took back the inventory and the photograph. 'I believe you. Now look at this. There's a note to say that they had to unscrew the bedroom door to get this shot.'

It was another photograph, also taken from the landing, but this time it showed the bed and the left hand side of the room. There was the window with its small panes and flimsy curtains but to the right of the window, between the bed and the wall, there was a massive old-fashioned wardrobe with a mirror in the door.

'You didn't mention a wardrobe, did you?'

'No, I must have forgotten it.'

'Do you remember it now?'

Milton paused for some time before answering. 'No.'

'Of course you don't, you were never in that room; all you saw of it you saw from the landing.' Hammond held up his hand. 'Now don't argue with me, it's a waste of time.' His manner was good humoured, almost bantering.

He seemed to be very pleased with himself and took time off to light a cigarette. Milton sank deeper into his chair and into depression.

'In our little chat upstairs you said that when you arrived, while you were in the passage by the front door, you heard a movement upstairs. Are you sure of that?'

'Quite sure. It was what made me call out again and then go upstairs. Otherwise I would have assumed that Christine had just slipped out to the shop or something like that.'

Hammond leaned across his desk and spoke with unusual gravity. 'But Christine was already dead. You know that now, whether you admit it or not, so if you heard somebody upstairs it was almost certainly the man who killed her. Of course it might have been a noise from next door but because of the watch I don't think it was. You were in the house with him.'

Milton was about to say something but stopped himself.

'You've remembered something?'

Milton said nothing.

'Out with it!'

'It was while I was standing on the stairs looking into the bedroom. I remember that something startled me and I turned to look at the other door; I think now that it must have been a sound from that room.'

Hammond was turning over another set of typed pages. 'This is what you said to us upstairs—all typed out, neat and tidy. Very efficient we are, on bloody paper.

'"I almost tumbled downstairs and into the kitchen where I vomited in the sink. I flushed the sink and went out into the hall. After a while I let myself out by the front door and closed it behind me."

'Is that right?'

'Yes.'

'You didn't think to wipe your finger-prints off the tap or the door knob?'

'Of course not, I was too upset, too terrified.'

Hammond nodded. 'Somebody went through that little house cleaning every surface which might have carried a print and he made a damn good job of it.'

Chapter Eleven

IT WAS NINE o'clock when he finally left the Central Police Station.

'I'll get one of our lads to run you back.'

'No, thank you, I'd rather walk.'

'Are you sure you're all right?'

'Quite all right, thank you.'

It had stopped raining and the sky had cleared; the moon was playing cat and mouse among the clouds, silvering their edges.

Milton felt numbed, incapable of experiencing any sensation or desire. He walked mechanically in the direction of the green and though he passed several bus stops he kept tramping steadily on through streets which, at this time, were almost deserted. Arriving at the green, he glanced across at Gladbrook House and glimpsed the porter in his green uniform, taking the air, outside the revolving doors.

He turned down by the bank, past the estate agent's and the café. He peered through the window of the café but could distinguish only the vague outlines of people sitting near the window. He walked as far as the bridge and there stopped, standing with his arms resting on the parapet. Below him the surface of the water in the canal was undisturbed by the slightest ripple.

He was in the position of a condemned man who, against all the odds, is granted a reprieve, and he felt utterly lost.

For twenty years he had lived with certain massive reservations, within strictly defined and narrow limits. For most of that time he had scarcely realised why the limits were there, but he had never questioned that they were necessary. Now he was like a cage-bird who has known no other life and is suddenly and cruelly set free.

He looked down at the dark, shining water and thought

how easy it would be to end it all. But that was an illusion. One needed courage of a kind he did not possess, or a complete lack of imagination.

He recalled the tramp who had been camping out in the squalor of 16 Bewdley Street. That was possible; he was not repelled by the notion. There was no need to start there; one could drift, sinking slowly, gently, to base-level.

He looked across again at the lights of Gladbrook House. Elizabeth and Jean were there and they wanted him back. He could go to the school and Bates would say: 'My dear chap! What you need is a term's rest. Sick-leave. You've undergone a traumatic experience. Take Jean and Elizabeth and go abroad for a good, long break. Don't worry about Elizabeth, she's bright, she could do an extra year if necessary—no problem. When you come back to us you'll be a new man!'

Bates could say that sort of thing as though he believed it. Perhaps he did. Instant therapy.

He shook his head.

He put his hand into his inside-breast pocket and brought out the envelope which contained Christine's photograph and her five letters. He held the photograph to the light from a street lamp and saw again her shy smile, head tilted to one side, and that curious warning signal in her expression. He had always been aware of it.

That link too was broken. He could look at her photograph without a tremor of emotion.

Somebody had killed her, she had been murdered, but she would not have been murdered if she had not been as she was. A natural victim. He had not killed her but he might have done.

He had suffered, had the other man? Either way he felt no rancour. Life is a pattern and any single thread can only twist and turn in the way which makes the pattern come right.

Tabb the ex-detective had looked at him oddly, in a way that he could not forget. He had interpreted that look as suspicion and he had even written in his absurd book: 'Tabb suspects'. He had fully expected that Tabb would communicate his suspicion to the police.

Yet Hammond had told him: 'He said you asked about police methods in general, not about any particular case.'

It was very quiet, only an occasional car swished across the junction by Gladbrook House. A double-decker bus came from the city, crossed the junction and cruised along Palmerston Road. He could follow its lights twinkling through the shrubs and bushes in the park.

Suspicion or fear? Fear? Why should Tabb fear him?

'And Sergeant Tabb—Tabby, we used to call him—he was almost like one of the family ... That's Tabby with the cornet. He was in the band, that's how we came to know him....'

'I wasn't on the case at the start, I'd been sent off on a course and I didn't get back until the investigation had been going for a week.'

Where was this course? How far away? When did it start? Could Tabb...?

The very idea was absurd. Nonsense!

'Never a friend of the family. I knew her father because we played in the same band; but there was no other connection—none.'

A neighbour had heard somebody arriving at the Wilsons' or the house next door in the small hours of Saturday morning.

There were no finger-prints.

'Somebody went through that little house cleaning every surface which might have carried a print and he made a damn good job of it.'

A car came slowly along Commercial Road but he took no notice until it stopped on the bridge behind him. It was a police car.

'Are you all right, sir?'

'Me? Yes, of course, just getting a breath of air.'

The young constable was still not happy. 'Do you live round here, sir?'

'Canal Street.'

The car moved on. Milton left his place by the parapet and walked slowly in the direction of the café.

'You didn't need to be a friend of the family to be upset by the girl's death and the way she died. I was still young

159

enough to be impressionable, not case-hardened. But I think anybody *who saw that girl lying there, naked, on the bed, would have felt as I did.*'

He pushed open the door of the café. Julie was behind the counter and she smiled at him. Three or four of the mackintosh brigade were still sitting at tables, reading their newspapers.

She drew some coffee.

'You look all in.'

'I'm all right.'

'Here, drink this.' She glanced up at the clock. 'We shall be closing in half-an-hour, then I'll take you home.'

He took his coffee to a table by the window.

'A-C-C-E-P-T-A-N-C-E'—that is the word.